In the factory, men fed rubber into the rolls in the blue haze of the daylight illumination, and everything was going smoothly. Till just before midnight.

Suddenly, a man near the door who had been working at a fast pace began to move very slowly.

Then, as if it were some sort of epidemic, one man after another along the production line slowed from normal pace to that somehow dreadful slow motion. Gradually all the slow-moving, seemingly drugged men began to tremble. And a few of them fell down.

It was the beginning of a mammoth epidemic, so mysterious and far-reaching, the Avenger must be summoned to check the spread of DEATH IN SLOW MOTION.

Books In This Series

By Kenneth Robeson

Published By

WARNER PAPERBACK LIBRARY

DEATH IN SLOW MOTION

by Kenneth Robeson

WARNER
PAPERBACK
LIBRARY

A Warner Communications Company

CHAPTER I

The Shivering Man

In the teeming beehive that is New York City, an old man shivered and looked ill.

Few people paid any attention, naturally. Down and out, a ragged bum, he was the kind of old man who would never draw a second glance from anyone.

If a skyscraper had fallen or an earthquake had opened a ten-foot crack down Broadway's entire length, everybody along the Atlantic seacoast would have dropped whatever he was doing to hear about it and observe it. Yet, a falling building or an earthquake would not have had the importance of this old bum's feebleness, could some prophet or seventh son of a seventh son have been around to discern that fact.

However, no such mythical person was nearby at the time; so he remained just a weakly moving old tramp beneath the notice of the passers-by.

He was on Waverly Place near Avenue of the Americas at the time and heading west.

He was about the most unsavory-looking character you'd wish to see. Of any age over sixty, he had straggly gray whiskers that looked like the moth-eaten fringe of an old rug. His watery brown eyes seemed to have a film of mist over them. He was fairly tall, but so stooped with age that he seemed a small man.

He was dirty, and his clothes obviously hadn't been off his feeble old frame for days, perhaps weeks. His shoes flapped a little as he shuffled along, because the soles were loose. And from the flapping fronts, you could now and then see a toe which had gone through its sock.

Altogether, not a spectacle to command interest, even though the old man might be in distress.

That he was in distress was apparent from his gait.

He shuffled a few steps and then leaned against a building wall for a moment, panting, with his hand to his ragged chest. He went on and almost sagged to his knees. He recovered, and tottered along again, west toward the Hudson River.

The old tramp was carrying a bundle as disreputable looking as himself.

A tattered newspaper was the wrapping of the bundle. From one end trailed the jagged ends of a few broken slats. Some bits of string trailed out, too. The old fellow had obviously been out gleaning in ash cans and the city streets, getting odds and ends that he might sell for a few pennies, and bits of wood for fuel with which to cook.

As he neared Avenue of the Americas, he seemed to become more and more ill. His spells of leaning against something for support were longer. His shivering grew more intense. His face, or what you could see of it behind the straggly whiskers and the dirt, had a gray-green look. About the shade of a lima bean.

Coming down Avenue of the Americas was a Negro.

He was tall, as thin as part of a split-rail fence, with feet like barges and with a sleepy-looking dull-witted face. He walked in the same manner as he talked. There was a lazy inclination to use just as little energy as possible for the result desired.

6

Josh Newton had graduated with high honors from Tuskegee Institute. He could, and did, talk with the crisp and precise diction of a college professor when he was among friends, and his brain and body were as fast as chain lightning when there was need for it.

But all this could be inferred in one simple phrase: he was a valued aid of Richard Henry Benson, known to an increasingly uneasy underworld as The Avenger.

Josh reached the corner of Waverly and Avenue of the Americas just about the same time as the old man. They were across Waverly Place from each other; but even across the street Josh's quick eye caught the old boy's distress.

He crossed in a hurry and went up to the aged tramp.

"Anything wrong with you-all?" he drawled. Josh, with strangers, scrupulously lived up to his lazy, no-account appearance.

"No," said the old man. "I'm all right."

His voice asked no favors. In fact, it was a harsh and repellent voice.

"Looks to me lak you's in trouble," drawled Josh. "Ah got a few nickels if some food'd help."

"I don't need food," snarled the old man. "Get away from me, will you?"

Josh stood back and viewed the trembling, tottering, ragged old ruin. And as he stepped back, the old man sank to his knees, floundered frantically to get up and could not make it.

Josh put an arm under the ragged shoulders.

"Get away from me, I tell you!" cried the old bum. "I'm all right—"

And saying this, he fell flat on his dirty, whiskery old face and lay in the dust of the sidewalk. He glared up at Josh, not unconscious, but unable to move a muscle.

So Josh picked him up and carried him to MacMurdie's

drugstore, which was a bare dozen steps from there and to which he had been going in the first place.

Fergus MacMurdie's drugstore looked like any other drugstore to the casual glance. The fact that it was not, that it was a highly unusual and significant place, was beginning to be harder and harder to conceal from an admiring public.

The front room of the store contained just what every medium-sized drugstore contains. But the rear room of the place was not at all what you'd expect to find.

It was huge, over twice as big as the store part, and it housed not one, but two complete laboratories.

Along one side was a great bench holding about all the paraphernalia ever devised for intricate and subtle electrical and radio experiments.

Along the other was an equally complete array of chemical apparatus.

The electrical half belonged to Algernon Heathcote Smith. The chemical apparatus, and the knowledge to use it as few chemists can use such equipment, belonged to MacMurdie.

Mac was in the front, regular part of the store when Josh entered with his tattered burden.

"Whoosh!" said the Scotchman. "What have we got here? A bundle for the laundry?"

The words were flippant, but the look in Mac's bleak eyes as he surveyed the old man was not.

He helped Josh with the old bum, his hands—which could form into bone mallets of fists—being very gentle about it. The lanky Negro and the tall, sandy-haired Scotchman took the shivering wreck into the rear room, with Mac nodding to the bright-faced boy who helped with the store to take any customers who might enter.

"Easy now, mon," said Mac, as the old fellow mumbled curses and snarling statements that he was all right and just wanted to be let alone. "Smitty, clear out that big chair, will ye?"

The electrical wizard who shared the dual laboratory with Mac had been at his bench, working with a new radio-tube idea.

Algernon Heathcote Smith was his name. But nobody —save occasionally MacMurdie—dared call him that. He was Smitty, and you'd better be careful about it. You would be careful, too, after one glance at him.

Smitty seemed to have come from a heroic age of thousands of years ago when men were men and ate saber-toothed tigers raw for breakfast.

He was six feet nine, weighed almost three hundred pounds, with every atom of it solid bone and muscle.

Topping this mountain of brawn was a moonface, looking more good-natured than intelligent, and in which were naïve-looking, china-blue eyes. You'd never have taken him for the electrical and radio wizard he was. And you'd never have guessed, probably, that he was another of the hair-trigger, dangerous aids of The Avenger.

Smitty jumped forward and took a bunch of miscellaneous junk off the tattered easy-chair mentioned by Mac. Then, as easily as if he had been but a feather, he picked the old man up and deposited him in it.

And the old tramp continued to snarl and curse and demand that they take him outside again and let him alone.

They made no move to do such a thing. They looked at the stubborn old coot with sympathy, and that was all. For they had no way of guessing the colossal significance hidden in the shivering distress of an aged hobo.

"May be 'tis malnutrition," said Mac. "Are ye hungry, mon?"

"No, I'm not hungry," snapped the old man, clawing at his straggly whiskers.

"Just how do ye feel?" inquired Mac, who was a pretty

9

good doctor, as well as a chemical and pharmaceutical genius. "Maybe if we heard the symptoms——"

"I feel perfectly all right," snarled the old bum, shivering.

"You certainly don't look it," rumbled the giant, Smitty.

"Maybe it's his heart," said Josh, abandoning his drawl and speaking like the educated man he was.

"It's not my heart!" rapped the old man. "It's nothing at all, I tell you. Let me——"

Mac put a stethoscope to his ragged breast. He looked at Smitty and shrugged.

"Heart's as good as ye could expect. This shiverin', now —'tis an odd thing." He stared at the old man. "Do ye have recurrent malaria, anythin' like that?"

"Will you let me go!" stormed the aged bum.

He tried to get up, and fell back into the chair, panting and shuddering.

Mac went over him. He found nothing definitely the matter, nothing that could be responsible for the man's condition. So he swung back to his first thought—malnutrition.

"We'll take ye to a restaurant and get a square meal under yer belt," he said cheerfully. "Then if that doesn't do the trick, we'll see about a clinic——"

Into the filmed brown eyes came shrewdness. The old bum had had but one thought in mind through all this— to be let alone. Evidently, there was a fierce spark of independence in him and he saw in Mac's words a chance to indulge it.

"All right," he snarled. "All right, I'm hungry, then. But I don't want to go to no restaurant. Take me home. I got some food at home."

Smitty half grinned at Josh.

"Be it ever so humble," he said in an aside. "You wouldn't think a guy like this had a home. I thought he was a foot-loose tramp."

"Probably a piano box somewhere," said Josh, also in

10

a low tone. "But it's to his credit that he has a place to live."

"All right, then," said Mac, soured by the snarling ingratitude of the man they were trying to help, "home it is. And where would that be?"

The aged relic told them. It was a number on a street that even Mac couldn't place for a moment, and then managed to locate. The difficulty with his memory was that it wasn't a street at all; it was an alley. Mac had never even known before that it had a name.

Smitty's car was at the curb. It was an ancient-looking coupe, but under the dull paint of the hood was a motor almost big enough to have powered a tugboat.

He and Josh went with the old man, stopped at the alley entrance because it was hardly big enough to get a car into. New York has practically no alleys. The few that do exist often date back a hundred years to a time when they were streets. Narrow, ill-lighted, noisome streets which were abandoned as thoroughfares as soon as the city grew.

The building to which the old man grudgingly let himself be helped, looked as old as the slimy alley. It was not big, a former carriage house perhaps. It was at a slant, indicating that it would sigh and collapse of its own weight some day. It was at the rear end of a narrow lot, with the shabby brick wall of a larger house cutting off all air and light. The brick house faced on the street just south of the alley.

A rear-house, this type of place is called. There are many of them in the land—rattletrap structures taking up the back half of a building lot and bringing in a few dollars extra rent. A slum building, usually, never getting sunlight, surrounded by higher, newer buildings as if it were in the bottom of a well. At least this one was like that.

There were two doors opening into the alley from this

squalid place. The old man hobbled to the right-hand one, clutching his pitiful bundle of gleanings from the streets under his left arm, fishing out a key with his right hand.

Growling and snarling, mumbling in his scraggy beard, he opened the door.

Smitty and Josh got one glimpse of the room inside. It was worse than the outside. Rags for a mattress, one broken chair and a propped-up table. Beside a rusted old stove was piled wood from old packing cases which could be used to cook with in summer and for heat in the winter.

That was all they saw.

"Just a minute, let me help you in," said Smitty kindly.

And the old man wobbled inside faster than they'd thought he could move. The ancient door slammed in their faces.

"Why, the—" began Josh.

But Smitty grinned.

"No charity case here," he said. "But I kind of admire the old boy. Won't take help, manages to keep together his own home, such as it is. He's got guts."

They looked at the door, shrugged and walked back down the alley toward where Smitty had left the car. And then Smitty lost some of his grin and looked as he felt— lazily curious.

"Did you notice the door next to his?" he said to Josh.

Josh shook his head.

"No! What about it?"

"The locks," said Smitty.

"Why wouldn't it have locks?" Josh said. "No matter what kind of a place a person has, it's home and he tries to protect it. Even that old bum had a lock of sorts on his door."

"Not like the locks on the door next to him," said Smitty. "Now that I think of it, they were certainly some locks! The biggest, heaviest, most expensive kind you can

12

buy. But the door itself looked as if a breath would break it in. Funny."

They got in the car and went back to the drugstore, quite naturally forgetting the whole affair.

CHAPTER II

Slow Death!

The factory appeared to be about a mile long, and it was four stories high. At night, with all the lights on and the very air humming with activity, it seemed to be an entire city all by itself.

In a way, that's what it was. It certainly housed a small city of workmen. And it had all the requirements of sanitation and supply and policing of a small city.

It was the central plant of the Wardwear Tire & Rubber Company, in Akron, Ohio.

The place was a maelstrom of activity. It was that way twenty-four hours a day, six days a week. That was because of war.

With war scattered over half the world and still spreading, the Wardwear Company was booming. Tires and a host of other rubber goods are essential in modern war. They are ordered by the million, and Wardwear was getting its huge share of the business.

So the mammoth factories buzzed and whirred with speeded-up assembly belts and wheels. And none of their plants was quite as busy as the central plant. And of this plant, no department was quite as busy as the crude-rubber department, where the raw rubber was converted into a more refined product which should presently go into the myriad molds and undergo the heat treatment to make tires.

It was in this department that it happened. And it started near the triple line of mammoth rolls into which the crude rubber was fed as the first of an unmerciful beating the stuff required for refining.

The rolls took the crude, masticated it with loud popping and snapping noises and spewed it out again. The rolls were like the steel lips of a giant; and the brownish raw rubber it flattened and worked was like chewing gum. The steel lips blew out the chewing gum into bubbles and awkward masses and seemed to suck it in again and chew it over like a cow chewing a cud, before finally giving it up.

The building trembled with the power of the rolls; and over all floated the impalpable dust, compounded of talc and rubber particles, that can never quite be cleared out of a rubber factory, even with the most powerful ventilating systems.

Men fed the raw rubber into the rolls in the blue haze of the daylight illumination, and everything was going smoothly. Till just before midnight. Then all of a sudden everything was not at all smooth!

Over near the inside wall, near the steel door that led to the power room, a man started to throw crude into a hopper. And his actions, abruptly, were very odd.

He had been working at a fast pace, keeping up with the machine in his charge. Now, suddenly, he began to move very slowly.

Very, very slowly! It was almost funny how slowly he moved. He began to look like a subject for a slow-motion picture. It was as if he had some young apprentice there and, by moving very slowly, an act at a time, was teaching him his job.

But there was no apprentice around. There was just the man, moving at about a fifth normal speed, taking three seconds or more to each step.

16

As if the thing were some sort of epidemic, it swept along the line, and finally all through the vast room!

One man after another slowed from normal pace to that somehow dreadful slow motion. In a couple of minutes the whole crew were going around like creatures in a dream with twenty pounds of lead on each foot, and on each hand, too.

The machines, however, did not slow down. They kept clanking along at their normal pace, and in a short time the discrepancy began to raise hell. The machines needed crude rubber fed to them and were not getting it. They began to clank emptily. And the trembling of the building increased till the vibration jarred your teeth.

The department foreman came into the place from the direction of the front office. He took one amazed, open-mouthed look at a crew of men, walking like badly co-ordinated robots; then he leaped, bellowing, for the nearest machine.

Whatever he was going to say was quickly muted.

Like the rest, he began to move more and more slowly, with his eyes glazed and dull and his motion weak. He went on with what he was starting to say, cussing out the man nearest him. And even his words were slow. It certainly didn't help what was supposed to have been crisp profanity to have a long silence between each syllable.

The thing would have been droll if it had not been so dreadful. In a moment it grew even more dreadful.

All the slow-moving, seemingly drugged men began to tremble.

Almost rhythmically, shudders swept through them as if they were very cold. To increase the illusion, even their teeth chattered with their violent shuddering. And a few of them fell down.

In the opened door of the power room, a figure was furtively standing. The figure had a sort of shield over its face, possibly to keep it from being identified. Like a minor demon in a little hell, this figure watched the stricken humans in the crude-rubber department.

Off to one side, one of the stricken men watched this figure. The man was dressed as the other workmen were dressed, but was not quite as they were. He was one of the company police, mingling with the run of the men, performing a multitude of duties outside the regular one of tending the machines.

This man was as affected as the rest; but with a tremendous call on his will power, he began to go toward the partly opened steel door with the masked face showing in the crack.

He moved as if he were a bear, awakened during hibernation time and hardly able to keep awake. It took him four or five minutes to traverse the thirty feet to the door.

Nearing the door, he started to draw the gun he carried under his coveralls.

Again, the effect would have been ludicrous if you hadn't sensed such life-and-death urgency in it.

The man's hand slowly went to his pocket, slowly came out with a flat .32 automatic, slowly began to level it. Of course the act was suicidal. It was like a fighter, in the ring, taking a full five seconds to draw back his arm and drive it forward again in a slow-motion left hook. What would the other man, not slowed, be doing all this time?

Exactly. And the man in the power-room doorway was acting just as that unslowed fighter would have acted.

He watched the gun come slowly out and slowly begin to level, almost as if he were amused. Then he drew his own gun.

He fired twice into the chest of the factory cop! And the cop fell. He even started to fall slowly, but then crashed to the floor in a fast heap.

The man in the doorway put up his gun, looked once more at the stricken department, then turned and walked out of sight.

Behind him, machines jammed and screamed, empty. More men began falling over in limp heaps! And presently the whole vast plant would stop humming because its supply was not coming out of this one vital department.

Death in slow motion seemed to have struck and, having struck, to linger still instead of moving on.

The man who had unconcernedly left the doorway after murdering the factory cop moved just as unconcernedly toward the big street exit of the place. In doing so, he stepped over the body of the assistant engineer, who had tried to put up an argument when the man first came in.

The assistant engineer lay with a neat blue hole in the right side of his head, and a gaping red crater on the left side of the skull where the bullet had torn out again!

It was now three minutes to twelve. The assistant's relief came in off the street, whistling, unaware of what had happened here.

He saw the man with the shield over his face.

Without a sound, like a well-trained watchdog that instantly sizes up a situation and acts accordingly, the man jumped.

It was so swiftly done that the man with the shield over his face hadn't time to get his gun out again. Snarling a little behind the shield, he battered a right and left into the engineer's face instead, swayed back with a return blow, then closed!

The masked man was very powerful. Disregarding a rain of blows, his hands went out and grabbed the engineer's throat. They tightened, like the coils of a snake.

The blows got weaker and fewer, then stopped. The engineer's face turned red, chalk-pale, purplish! Came a moment when his movements were convulsive and terrific, and then a following moment when they ceased entirely.

Calmly, coldly, the man with the masked face dropped

the stark body and went on to the exit. Three had died under his hand, now.

At the curb were lines and lines of cars, belonging to employees. They were parked diagonally, with their noses to the curb; but a few with the radiators pointing outward because they had been backed in.

In one of these parked cars, all of which were dim and without lights, two men sat in the front seat, slouched down so that it took a sharp eye to realize that this sedan wasn't empty, too. And this was one of the cars that had been backed in so that it could be instantly driven away into the night.

The man who had killed three of his fellows almost in as many moments went to this car, taking the shield off his face as he did so. His features were revealed, and a natural wonder sprang up as to why he didn't wear something over them all the time.

The jaw was heavy and brutish. The eyes were little, hard pinpoints of black under heavy black eyebrows. There were scars on cheeks and throat. The mouth was a mere gash under a smashed nose. Very often, murderers don't look like murderers at all. This man did.

One of the men in the car opened a rear door for him. This man stared his question. The fellow who had come from the power plant nodded an affirmative answer.

There had been no words spoken. And still with no exchange of words, the car sped off into the blackness. It was as if the men were all deaf-mutes, able to convey meanings only with looks and signs.

Ten blocks away, a police car screamed past them, on its way to the Wardwear plant. The sedan moved sedately on at a law-abiding speed. Another cop car, and another, followed.

They had no way of knowing that this innocent-looking sedan had anything to do with the now-distant factory. All they knew was that a call had come from a frantic manager about murder and a queer slow motion of the workers in the crude-rubber department—and of a whole vast plant brought to a standstill by some mysterious blow.

CHAPTER III

Deaf-and-Dumb Murder!

The glittering town car held a precious human cargo indeed. The four men in the capacious back were worth about a hundred million dollars.

They were rubber-factory owners, barons of Akron, and held executive positions with the American Rubber Institute, that association of manufacturers which molds prices, opinions and foreign policies in addition to molding rubber.

They were Thomas Wardwear, Anthony Hillyard, Abel Quill and Michael Moribunce. Wardwear was the richest and most important, but the others didn't have to look up very far to his eminence, at that.

In front with the chauffeur was a fifth man of this party, but he was a small cinder heap compared to a mighty mountain. He was cheaply dressed and had gnarled, work-torn hands. He sat there shivering like a chilled dog and moving in a curiously slow fashion when he wanted to shift position. Several times, his shoulder bumped the window upright because he couldn't get his arm up in time to brace himself when a curve was rounded.

This man was in the rubber business, too. But at the bottom. He worked for Wardwear, in the crude-rubber department.

As the big machine passed a corner newsstand, the boy was calling forth the evening papers. "Extra! Read all about it! Another Akron factory—"

Another one. That was the second.

Wardwear's main plant had been paralyzed by the defection of the crude department. But Abel Quill's whole factory had suffered the same mysterious slow-motion, shivering, enfeebling malady seven hours later, just before the day shift went on.

So the four men had chartered a plane for New York, bringing the sample workman from Wardwear's plant with them.

Now, in the big car, they were bound for Bleek Street, and, they hoped and prayed, deliverance from a thing that seemed more dangerous and mysterious every time they thought of it.

A hundred million dollars or more, humbly on its way to Bleek Street. But from looking at that street, you'd never guess it could be a mecca for such men.

It was a short block in lower Manhattan. The north side of Bleek Street was taken up entirely by the windowless back of a great, concrete storage building. In the center of the south side were three narrow, red brick, three-story buildings, looking old and dingy and shabby.

And all of the south side was either owned by or under long lease to one man. So that this one man, in effect, owned the block.

This man, whose headquarters were the three red brick buildings which had been thrown into one, was Richard Henry Benson—The Avenger.

It was to see The Avenger that these important men in the rubber industry were going.

The town car reached the corner of Bleek Street and turned west toward its dead end. It stopped in front of the center entrance of the red brick buildings.

24

Over this entrance was a small unobtrusive sign. It had dull gilt letters on it, and the letters said:

JUSTICE, INC.

"This is it," said Wardwear, a square-bodied man with rimless glasses.

"Come along" said Moribunce to the factory workman beside the chauffeur.

The man got out. He was very ill. That could be seen at a glance. His pallor was chalky, and he was shivering, as if he were very cold, though the day was warm.

He moved with curious, eerie slowness. His foot descended and touched the pavement like a scene in a slow-motion picture. His body followed with equal slowness; it took him a full minute to cross the sidewalk, even with two of the rubber magnates helping him impatiently.

Wardwear pushed the buzzer in the vestibule.

There was a moment of silence and inaction. During that moment, though they did not know it, the five men were under scrutiny.

Upstairs there was a small television set, designed by Smitty, that was constantly on. This revealed whoever was in the vestibule.

A soft hum sounded and the vestibule door opened. The five men went slowly—for the benefit of the slow-moving workman—up two flights of stairs which were very richly carpeted and whose walls were draped with tapestries worth a fortune.

Quill was in the lead. He started to tap at the door at the top of the stairs, but there was another soft hum and the door opened by itself.

The five strode in.

They saw a tremendous room, taking up the top floor of the three buildings in one.

They saw a Scotchman with outstanding ears, dim freckles under a coarse skin, sandy ropes of eyebrows over bleak blue eyes, and sandy-reddish hair in a rough thatch.

They saw a man who was a veritable giant, with a torso so muscled that his arms would not hang straight.

They saw a demure, slim, small blond girl who looked as delicate as porcelain and twice as fragile. Of course, they did not know that this was Nellie Gray, blond little bombshell who could handle most strong men with her ability at boxing, wrestling and jujitsu.

One important member of The Avenger's crime-fighting crew who was not present was Cole Wilson, the young mechanical-engineering genius who was in Washington, aiding the government on an important defense project.

Then they saw the personage they guessed at once to be the leader here.

The man was seated behind a huge desk, but even seated he gave an impression of vast physical power and unbelievable quickness. And this was odd because he had a very average-sized body—no more than five feet eight in height and weighing about a hundred and sixty-five pounds.

His face was handsome, but that didn't impress you as much as the strength of character portrayed in his features. Features that told at a glance that here sat a natural leader of men. And from this face burned basilisk eyes so colorless that they seemed to be mere holes into which you could peer endlessly at a world of fog and gray ice.

But even as they looked at him, these men who had come to seek his aid knew that Dick Benson, regardless of the stories they had heard of his genius, his experience in most any given field, his adventures in every corner of the earth, was a very young man. A man who was already a figure beyond the equal of any other, at an age when most men are looking vaguely about for a foothold in life.

"Mr. Benson?" said Wardwear.

The head, topped by the virile shock of coal-black hair, nodded.

"We are——"

"You are Thomas Wardwear, Abel Quill, Michael Moribunce and Anthony Hillyard," said The Avenger, his face expressionless in its usual calmness. "I have been expecting some such visit, gentlemen."

"Then you know about the second factory catastrophe?"

In the far corner of the room was the latest in teletypes, and over this flashed all the world's news. Thus, Dick Benson knew of the death of an obscure laborer almost as soon as it happened, let alone news of such importance as the halting of a great factory.

But he did not explain; he only nodded again.

"With the trouble at my plant," said Wardwear, "we all might have thought that some distressing but perfectly natural accident had occurred, and would have set about trying to correct it by natural means. But when, in only a few hours, a similar thing happened to another similar plant, and similarly wrecked its output for an indefinite number of days, we all began to think——"

He stopped, and Hillyard took it up with the one dread word:

"Sabotage!"

Quill nodded.

"Wardwear's factory stopped by tragedy in the crude department, which is enough to keep all wheels from turning. My own whole factory affected——"

"Your whole plant?" Dick asked quickly.

"That's right."

"And in your case, Mr. Wardwear," said The Avenger, "just one department was affected?"

"Yes," said Wardwear rather impatiently. "But I don't see what difference it makes how much of a factory is affected when the result is the stopping of the entire plant."

"Possibly none," murmured Benson. He looked at the

27

fifth man, the ailing workman from Wardwear's factory. In his colorless, dreadful eyes was a little less iciness. There was a trace of impersonal kindness and sympathy.

"This is Robert Maschek, from my crude-rubber department," said Wardwear. "He saw the whole mysterious business. I thought you might be interested—"

"I would be very interested," Dick cut him off, "to hear all about it. Will you tell me, Mr. Maschek?"

The man took a slow step nearer the desk. His dully suffering eyes rested on Dick's face. And he began to talk, with a pause between each word, since his tongue and larynx seemed as subject to the queer slow-motion disease as his other muscles.

He told of the odd slow-up, of machines jamming and racing emptily when human hands no longer kept up with them. He told of his own slow surprise and that of the other men, at the jamming, because none had realized that he was moving more slowly than usual.

And as he talked, he shivered like a dog after an ice-water bath, and there were green-gray tints in his chalky face.

He told of the murder of the factory cop by the man with the hidden face at the doorway.

As he talked, Nellie Gray stared with almost tearful sympathy at him. The giant Smitty and the Scot, Mac, stared with equal sympathy, but with perplexity in their eyes, too. Because this shivering wreck of a man reminded them of something that for the moment they could not place.

At the end of his account, The Avenger turned back to the four magnates. What was in his mind could not have been read in his calm face nor in his icy, colorless eyes.

"I'll do what I can to solve this, gentlemen," he said. And the four sighed with relief. They could not know that this man would have done what he could anyhow, whether or not they had come to see him and ask for help.

Rubber goods, particularly tires, are part of the sinews of war. With war all over the world, and even talk of the inevitability of America's own entrance, anything affecting the rubber output is a sinister thing to be instantly investigated.

The five went out. And Benson rose from the chair behind his desk.

With the move, you saw at once just how fast and how strong that average-sized body was. He seemed to flow, rather than move, so swift and smooth were his movements.

He stepped to one of the front windows and stared out and down. In his right hand were several small glass capsules, small enough to be dropped between the nickel-steel, bullet-proof slats which were set in the masonry to imitate ordinary Venetian blinds.

In those capsules was a gas of MacMurdie's invention that could instantly induce unconsciousness in anyone near whom they broke.

The Avenger did not think it probable that men like these four would be attacked in broad daylight on his own street. But he was taking no chances. If anybody were lurking around the entrance, Dick meant to put them out of the running.

He saw the four go out the door. And there was no one nearby. The men got into the town car, with the workman getting in beside the chauffeur.

The pale eyes saw the chauffeur slam the doors, reach for the gear-shift lever, and then, after a little pause, saw the car start to turn smoothly around to go back out the street.

"Smitty! Mac!" Dick Benson's voice positively crackled. "After that car! Nellie! To the elevator with me. You and I will follow in a car while Mac and Smitty go on foot!"

Mac and Smitty were already thundering down the

29

stairs. They had not stopped to ask what their leader had seen, and they had obeyed commands instantly.

What The Avenger had seen had been a very small thing, indeed.

He had seen that when the chauffeur reached for the gear-shift to start to turn, he had fumbled to the right for a gear-shift lever—and there was no such lever! The car had its shift lever on the steering column, in the new style.

That small move instantly told that the man was unfamiliar with the car he was supposed to drive for his living, which was very odd. And The Avenger's quick brain had as instantly sensed peril.

It had sensed it truly!

CHAPTER IV

Mysterious Malady

There was normally no traffic on Bleek Street. Inasmuch as only Justice, Inc., was on it, only people wanting to see The Avenger entered. Usually! But there was traffic on it, now.

Smitty and Mac burst out of the street door, looked to the right and saw three cars beside the town car, halfway between the entrance and the end of the block.

The phony chauffeur was stopping the town car even as The Avenger's two aids began to race toward the tangle. And the three sedans began to pour out men.

The sedans had been crowded to capacity. About twenty men were milling around when the cars had emptied.

They were milling around that town car!

Smitty and Mac, getting close, saw the chauffeur tugging to get the rear door open; they saw the four princes of the rubber industry inside frantically hanging on and trying to keep them closed till they could throw the locks.

Evidently, they snapped the locks because the chauffeur suddenly stopped trying to yank the doors and took a heavy wrench from his pocket instead. He smashed the glass.

Meanwhile, the score of men from the sedans were acting rather strangely. There was not one sound from

31

any of them. No word, no yell, nothing. Instead, two of them pointed at the man in the front seat beside the driver's seat, and some more of them nodded. Then three of them aimed guns and shot that man. They then joined the chauffeur at the rear door.

Mac and Smitty went berserk!

Murdering a sick man, seated and defenseless, in cold blood! They wanted nothing more than to get to close quarters with these deaf-mutes, or whatever they were that acted so silently by making sign language to one another.

But Mac wasn't so wild as to have lost all his wits. As the two charged into a group just becoming aware of their approach for the first time, Mac's right arm made throwing motions. And from his right hand shot a half dozen of the little glass capsules containing the gas.

One of the men in the gang suddenly bent far down, as if trying to roll a pea with his nose for an election bet. But he kept on bending down till finally he fell on his face, with his nose plowing along the sidewalk.

Three more of the men sagged, and half a dozen reeled as they moved away from that spot.

They got to the other side of the car and began shooting. But they had not been fast enough with their guns.

Mac raced around the car toward the rear. Smitty didn't race anywhere. He just jumped!

The gigantic form, which you'd think would have been muscle-bound but which was actually as lithe as a boy's, went over the hood of the town car like a track man over a hurdle. Two men shot over backward like tenpins, as the giant's smashing feet began the battle before even he had hit the street.

They couldn't shoot, then, without drilling each other. For, at once, the big fellow was the center of a pulling mob, like a brawny half-back wading down a football field with a dozen men on him!

Smitty's vast fists pistoned in and out like something

propelling huge flywheels in a power plant. And with each blow, a man folded up. And it was possible that a few would never unfold again, for men like Smitty—what few of them there are—can kill with their bare fists.

Clubbing at the colossus with their guns, the deaf-and-dumb crew started to get him down; then Mac got around the car and waded in from the rear!

His fists, at the end of his long, wiry arms, were like ivory mallets. Cartilage and flesh gave before them. More men went down. But it was still five or six to two, and the outcome of the battle would have been problematical, save that at that moment The Avenger's car shot up the ramp from the basement garage, over the sidewalk to the street, and charged toward the struggling knot like a runaway locomotive.

Dick had taken the sedan in case the town car got out of the street before Mac and Smitty could get it afoot. He used it now like a tank.

The gang scrapping with Mac and Smitty heard the roar of the motor and hopped nimbly to right and left. But they were not to be run down.

The Avenger's steely, slim hand pressed something that looked like a horn button but was not a horn button, and from the grilled radiator shield came a blinding white cloud. It was an anaesthetic. It enveloped the town car and the struggling men. Most of them fell, including Mac and Smitty. But a few reached the three waiting sedans.

The cars roared off, leaving a dozen men behind.

There was the distant scream of police sirens. The cops were coming; the four rubber barons were safe. And that was all Smitty and Mac knew as they sank into the deep sleep induced by the white mist The Avenger had ejected from the front of his car.

At Mac's drugstore, hours later, they were feeling fine again, save for some lumps raised by the deaf-and-dumb crew. Feeling fine—and very thoughtful.

Both were thinking the same thing, as both remembered the way that workman had looked in the Bleek Street headquarters. The unfortunate fellow who had been shot by the gang.

"Shiverin'," mused Mac aloud. "The mon was tremblin' all the time. And verra weak. That colorin', and the draggy way he moved——"

"Seems to me I've seen somebody like that before," said Smitty.

It was obvious from Mac's look that he'd gotten precisely the same thought at precisely the same time. The men stared at each other, bleak blue eyes into china-blue eyes.

"That old tramp!" breathed Smitty.

Mac nodded emphatically.

"The same colorin'. The same shiverin', though not quite as noticeable a slow motion. Smitty, we may have something here. Do we call the chief?"

Smitty thought a minute, then shook his head.

"It's a pretty thin hunch, Mac," he said. "Why in the world would there be any connection between an old bum in New York and a couple of rubber factories in Akron, Ohio? Let's just nose around a little on our own hook. We'll almost surely find nothing at all—but it's an idea."

They went on foot to the place where Smitty had taken the aged hobo a couple of days ago, because it was only a few blocks from the store. It was getting dark as they reached the mouth of the dismal, narrow alley. They stared down at the front of the shabby, leaning rear-house.

"Poor old guy," said Smitty. "Pretty bad to have to live in a joint like that."

He gnawed at his lip. "And yet," he went on, "there must be something worth while looking after in that place, or else somebody's crazy."

"Huh?" said Mac.

"The locks," said Smitty, pointing to the door on the left of the old man's door. "Those great big, heavy new locks on that door. They weren't put on there for nothing."

Mac shrugged, and the two went to the aged tramp's door.

Smitty knocked. The frail door rattled back and forth as if just the giant's tap would break it in. But there was no answer. Smitty tried the door and found it locked, though the lock on this door was not at all like the complicated devices on the other alley door.

"Not at home," said Mac. "So now what?"

"We might wait for him a few minutes," rumbled the giant.

On each side of the miserable shack was the back end of a large, cheap apartment building, running from street in front to alley in the rear. But on each side, between rear-house and apartment house, was a very narrow runway.

Mac and Smitty waited in the left one, and then they suddenly heard steps from behind them.

They turned. A woman was coming toward them. It was necessary for the two to go out into the alley so the woman could get down the narrow runway.

They saw her for a moment as she came out. An elderly woman, heavy-set, squat, large-footed, dressed in clothes that must have been worn for a long, long time, and yet were reasonably clean. Thousands of her kind patiently clean the city's many office buildings, trailing scrub brushes and pails full of gray water behind them.

She glanced heavily, incuriously, at them and went down the alley to the street. Mac and Smitty stepped back into the narrow passageway.

They waited quite a little while.

"We might as well come back again tomorrow," growled Smitty, "or just leave and stay left. This is a crazy idea anyhow. There can't possibly be any connection—"

Steps sounded in the alley. It was as if someone had left the old man's door, or the door next to it, and the two hadn't heard the door opening. Both popped into the alley.

A man was coming from the narrow runway on the other side of the rear-house.

"They duck in and out like rabbits in a maze," complained Mac. "There must be a couple of stairways and doors in the back of this joint, too, to feed the top-floor rooms."

Smitty only said, "Let's get this guy and ask a few questions."

It was easy to catch up to this second person to leave the rear-house, for the man had a twisted leg and walked quite slowly.

He turned in surprise and a little fear as he heard the two behind him. But the fear left when he saw the amiable look on gigantic Smitty's moonface.

"Hello," said Smitty. "You live in that house?"

"Yes," said the man. "Top floor, left-hand side. My name is Mason," he added.

"We wanted to see the old fellow on the ground floor," Mac said. "Do you know if he is in?"

"No, I don't," said Mason. "He's a quiet old chap. I never know whether he's in or out. Are you friends of his?"

"We were afraid he was sick," evaded Smitty.

"Come to think of it," said the man, "Old Mitch has looked badly for several days."

"Old Mitch?"

"That's all the name I know," said the man with the twisted leg, apologetically. "Everybody just calls him Old Mitch. For Mitchell, I suppose."

"Say," blurted Smitty impulsively, "you seem a cut above a joint like that rear-house. How is it you live in there?"

The man smiled. And the smile took years off his face. He had looked about fifty before. Now he seemed no

36

more than in his thirties. He looked meek and beaten and humble—but not old.

"I have lived in better places," he said. "But I have to have extra money, right now, and a bookkeeper doesn't make much. There is a Mrs. Mason. I think she can come home from Arizona pretty soon, with cured lungs. But in the meantime"—he waved his hand—"I live here so she can stay in a sanitarium there."

There were no heroics in his tone, just a statement of fact. Mac and Smitty thanked him for his courtesy, and he went on.

"Now?" said Mac disgustedly.

But it was Smitty's turn to be stubborn.

"Make it just fifteen minutes more. Then we'll blow."

Thirteen of the fifteen minutes passed, and they saw the object of their visit.

At the alley entrance toiled a bent, aged figure with a ragged bundle in its arms. From the end of the bundle trailed a few bits of string and also protruded the jagged ends of broken wood for fuel.

"Here we go," said Smitty starting toward the old man. But Mac caught his arm.

Another figure appeared at the alley entrance. This one was that of a younger and well-dressed man.

"What in the world would he want with that old bum?" snapped Smitty suspiciously.

What the young, well-dressed fellow wanted was nothing good, apparently.

He said something in a loud, angry tone to the old man, and the old fellow cowered back.

Then the man the bookkeeper had called Old Mitch said something in a low, placating tone. But it didn't placate.

"Why, you old fool—" Mac heard the young fellow snarl. Then there was the sound of a blow and the old man sprawled piteously in the alley.

With one impulse, Mac and Smitty raced for the young bully. But they didn't get him. There was the sound of a motor, and a cheap but new roadster flashed away as they got to the street. The young fellow was driving it.

They helped the old fellow up—and they got the same snarling, querulous ingratitude they'd received before.

"Lemme alone. I'm all right. Lemme be, I tell you! I can take care of myself."

The old fellow was shaken from the blow but otherwise he looked all right. Mac took special care to see that, without letting Old Mitch know that he was being given the once-over.

He wasn't shivering any more. His color was not good, but at least it was no longer that bean-green shade. And he didn't move any more slowly than any other man.

"Lemme go, dang it!" Old Mitch snarled.

So Smitty let him go. But he looked after the cheap new roadster with hard eyes.

"I got the license number," he said. "I'll phone it in to the police and let them give him a going over. I'll teach that guy to hit an old, defenseless man!"

"No!" snapped Old Mitch instantly. "No! I . . . you can't do that!"

"Why not?" demanded Smitty curiously.

"Because . . . you . . . I don't want you to. I can take care of myself, I tell you. I'll fight my own battles!"

"Good for you," approved Smitty. "But just the same, I'll give that young fellow something to remember me by."

"I won't let you look him up!" raved Old Mitch, seeming ready to literally froth at the mouth. "If you haul him in, I'll swear he never touched me! See?"

"That sounds," said Smitty quietly, "as if you knew him."

"I do," said Old Mitch.

His shoulders drooped and showed the full weight, and more, of his years and feebleness.

"He is my son!" he said, with a volume of unspoken grief in the tone of voice. "I . . . I don't want to be a burden on him; so he goes his way and I go mine."

"Except for once in a while," said Mac hotly, "when he drops around to get pennies or something from you—and knocks you down!"

"He is my son," said the old man wearily. "I would never permit charges to be lodged against him."

He turned and went laboriously down the alley, bundle of discarded wood scraps and other bits of junk tightly held under his ragged old arm.

CHAPTER V

Strike Three

In Akron, Ohio, two rubber factories had been paralyzed by the mysterious business of their workers abruptly turning into slow-motion automatons.

The factories stayed paralyzed. No workman would enter the crude-rubber department of Wardwear's plant, or any part at all of the Quill factory. They were afraid they would get the same queer malady that had afflicted the other workmen.

The fear was justified. That malady was deadly!

Several dozen of the workmen had already died. Of the rest, a score or more were at death's door. And the balance were very sick men and getting worse.

Some kind of anaemia, the doctors said vaguely. And it was an anaemia that grew worse instead of better. It looked as if every man affected, and there had been hundreds, was going to die sooner or later.

In the two plants, watchmen hired for their almost crazy courage were on guard to keep the vacant shops from being looted. Nothing happened to the watchmen, which would seem to argue that it was safe to go back, now.

But just the same, no workman could be induced to enter the places and start the machines again. So two plants were out of the running.

And a third blow, had anyone known it, was in the process of paralyzing another plant.

This time it was in New York.

Down near the Hudson River, a light closed truck left a clattering machine shop that specialized in machine tools and dies. The truck had a load of jigs and dies for the Manhattan Rubber Gasket Company.

This company was small—its plants employed only a hundred and four men all told—but it was highly important. It made only one thing—various rubber gaskets. It was made immensely important by one type of gasket now being turned out in quantity lots.

This gasket was made from a secret formula and by a secret process for the tubing of ships, notably warships and coast-guard cutters. Just one small part of the labyrinth of machinery in a ship. But it is impossible to overrate the importance of that one part.

The little plant was working night and day to turn out an order of those gaskets for war use.

The truck went east on Canal Street, north on one of the avenues, east again. There is a lot of trucking on the crosstown streets; so the truck went slowly.

There was a man at the wheel, and a man with a gun sat beside him. The man with the gun was smoking idly. He pointed suddenly ahead and to the right.

"Fight," he said.

"Looks like it," said the driver.

Three men were on the sidewalk. They said no word to each other, but two were glaring at the third. And as the men in the truck watched, one of the two reached out with his hand, planted it in the third man's face and pushed.

The third man came back swinging and knocked one of the other two backward off the sidewalk, directly in front of the truck.

The driver stopped with a screeching of brakes, and the

purpose of the fight was immediately apparent. It was just to stop the truck.

At once, the two men left on the walk leaped for the right-hand side of the truck! The man with the gun, thoroughly alarmed, snapped it up—and was felled by a blackjack. The driver started to swing a hunk of metal rod which he kept in the cab for self-defense. But he was clubbed down by the third man, who had slipped up to the other side.

That was all there was to it.

The three heaved the two slack bodies into the truck, then climbed in themselves. The one who took the wheel was a young fellow, excellently dressed, with narrowed eyes and a thin gash of a mouth.

There was some yelling and commotion around, by then; and the young fellow, looking as if only faintly annoyed, drove off fast. The truck went down a street on which was a large old building, just vacated for a wrecking crew to tear down a little later.

When the truck emerged down this street, some minutes later, there were two men in the front again, dressed in the clothes of the two who had originally been there. And this time the young fellow was not driving. He sat beside the man who had been knocked in front of the truck to stop it and directed him where to turn.

He did it by signals, as if the driver were a deaf-mute.

The truck drew up before heavy gates in front of a small yard, almost completely filled by the neat building of the Manhattan Gasket Company.

At this gate were two guards, for, as has been said, this small factory was immensely valuable. The guards motioned to the two men in the truck to get down. They did so. And the guards searched them thoroughly. They went through the truck, too.

"O.K.," grunted one. "Nothing on 'em there shouldn't be."

43

The two got back in and drove the truck to the loading platform.

Down the building wall from this platform, a hundred yards or less, was the employees' entrance. The young fellow started walking casually toward this.

In the yard were piles of supplies and crates. And among the crates was a ragged old figure, gleaning from the littered ground bits of things he might use or sell for a few pennies.

It was Old Mitch.

The old man had a round of such places he went to, and he was allowed to hang around by tolerant, sympathetic guards or watchmen who respected the old boy's guts in his determined effort to keep alive without charity. They even let him salvage scrap metal occasionally, though this was forbidden.

He had come in here for bits of wood or whatever he could get, and now he looked up and saw the young fellow who had treated him so brutally the night before.

With hate in his eyes, Old Mitch glided behind a crate. The young man came on. Old Mitch picked up a rusted length of pipe and balanced it, but then let it drop. He only hid, while the young man passed the crate that sheltered him.

The young fellow opened the door of the employees' entrance.

There was a man there in grease-grimed shopcoat. He looked furtively around, then stared aggressively at the young fellow.

"All right, all right," the latter rasped. "Have a look. It's all yours, later."

He flipped open a wallet bulging with bills.

The man's eyes glistened. "Gimme!" he said.

The young fellow reached under his coat and took out a package the size of a book. He gave it to the man, who disappeared inside with it.

The young fellow waited for about thirty seconds, then, smiling, walked inside himself. He was back in about three minutes.

Over at the loading platform, the final contents of the truck were being taken out. It was just about time to go.

The young fellow's smile grew a little set as the seconds passed. He held his hand over the outside of his coat pocket, over a ragged, burned hole.

The employee came back.

"It's done," he said. "Now give it to me."

"Sure," said the smiling young man. "Here it is."

He reached into his pocket with the hole and then jammed something as deeply into the man's abdomen as he could. There was a muffled sound.

A gun shot through a thick garment and with its muzzle buried four or five inches in abdominal flesh, as in a pillow, makes much less noise than you'd think.

One of the guards turned. At the loading platform, one of the workmen looked up as he slammed the truck's rear door.

The young fellow, smiling, was shutting the door of the employees' entrance. He was the perfect picture of a man having had a few words with a friend who worked here and now, having said good-by, was turning with a little smile to leave.

The guards waved indifferently as the truck went back out the yard gate with the two men in it. And after that, the guards thought no more about trucks at all because all hell broke out in that factory!

There were screams and yells. There was, even audible on the outside, the sounds of machinery racing emptily or else jamming because the human hands tending them suddenly failed to keep up with them.

The guards ran to the employees' entrance. They jerked

open the door. And they saw what the young man had smilingly closed the door on.

The man who had received the bundle from him lay on the floor with his life running from a ghastly crater in his stomach.

One guard stayed with the man, and that one was lucky because he only got a touch of it. The other ran on, and about seventy hours later he was to die for that!

He burst past the time clock and into the factory room. There he stopped as if he had run into a wall—and stared with bulging eyes.

He saw a few men on the floor, limp. He saw others walking around like nightmare figures with lead tied to hands and feet, so slow, so slow, seconds to each step.

The women's screams were coming from the general office room just beyond; and the guard started toward the door to that, reasoning that there must have been a holdup in the front office.

It would have been funny to see the guard if it had not been so dreadful.

He started on the run. He continued that way, only his running grew slower and slower till it was not as fast as an average walking pace.

He took long, running strides, but they occurred at slow-motion intervals. He swung his arms to aid his speed, but they swung very, very slowly, like pendulums frozen in motion.

He reached the office door, after a long time, but did not get through.

He was one of the men they found unconscious on the floor a little later, when police—with gas masks against the unknown peril—came in to the rescue.

One hundred and thirty-nine people stricken, this time, because here the whole place had fallen under the malevolent spell, plant and office and everything else.

One hundred and thirty-nine people; and the doctors talked vaguely of some kind of anaemia. As if anaemia could hit like a bolt of lightning, in only a few minutes!

CHAPTER VI

Blood in a Bottle

The police sergeant, the medical examiner and the three plain-clothes men stared at Dick Benson with an awe born of the fact that they knew so much about him.

"Think we ought to keep on using these masks while we look around?" the sergeant asked The Avenger.

"I certainly do," was Dick's response.

"Think there's something in the air here that did this to all these folks, huh?"

"I don't know," said The Avenger, his pale eyes as brilliant as agates with lights behind them.

"If it was something in the air," persisted the sergeant, "what kind of thing would it be? Disease germs?"

"I haven't the faintest idea," said Benson.

And they had all stared at The Avenger in astonishment.

By now, Dick Benson was well known to every police force in the United States, and to those in large cities all over the world. He was particularly well known in New York.

The cops in New York had built legends around this man. He could do anything. He was all-powerful. He was fabulous and knew everything.

They forgot that even The Avenger was, after all, a

human being and that no human, no matter how much of a genius, can know everything.

So they were amazed and a little taken aback when, now, Benson admitted that he hadn't the faintest idea what could cause this grim carnage in a factory.

To his scientific mind, versed in mysterious illnesses and subtle crime, this thing seemed completely impossible. The more you knew of such matters, the more you would swear it was impossible.

Yet, it had happened three times to three factories in a vital industry.

"Maybe masks are necessary; maybe they're not. Anyhow, keep them on while we look around," he told the police quietly.

He viewed the dead body of the employee at the entrance, taking less than a minute to do it. Then he went on to the offices.

For a time, in the general chaos of the plant, a secondary crime that had been committed had gone undiscovered. Then a detective had questioned one of the girls from the office, who had been taken to the roof and lay there, now, not so much affected by this eerie slow-motion death from thin air. And the girl had said something that drew Washington and the entire Secret Service into the case at once.

She had said something about a smiling young man coming into the office with a receipt book which he said the vice president in charge of purchases was to sign. He had gone into the vice president's office, and the girl had gone to the door because, being the vice president's secretary, she hadn't been sure she should admit the man.

Then the whole place had fallen apart and gone crazy with the slow-motion peril. She had been as terrified, and had screamed as loudly, as the rest. But she had still seen the young man, mask over his face, leap for the office vault.

50

The vice president had staggered after him, had been shot for his pains, and then the young man had run from the office toward the employees' entrance.

The Avenger looked at the body of the vice president. The abdomen of the dead man was a gory ruin, blown half away.

"Gun jammed deep in the flesh to deaden the sound," mused Benson, eyes with that strange, frightening brilliance. "Same as the man at the door. It is almost certain that the same man, the smiling young fellow, killed them both. And it is equally probable that he caused this disaster, by what means I still can't even guess."

He didn't inquire into the nature of the thing that had been taken from the executive's vault. He knew. Washington had known the instant the police had phoned.

The thing that had been taken was the secret formula for the rubber of which those special gaskets for warship tubing had been made. A thing as vital in wartime as the blueprints for the latest bombsight, though not nearly as spectacular.

The Avenger went out to the one guard left at the gate.

This man was not feeling so well. He had gotten one touch of the queer doom that had overtaken the rest in the building. But he was saying nothing about it, staying around to help if possible because he felt that all this was his fault.

A guard ought to keep such things from happening. And he hadn't.

"The only thing that entered this yard and approached the building was that supplies truck?" The Avenger asked.

"That's right," said the guard.

"Describe it, please."

"One-and-a-half-ton truck, closed, dark-brown, with

Atlantic Tool and Die Company lettered on it. Fairly new. Two men in it."

There was a phone at the gate, in a little house of its own like a police call box. Benson used it as such, getting in touch with headquarters. His voice was calm but vibrant, and he seemed two feet taller than his actual size.

"Have two men been found dead or hurt in the vicinity of the Manhattan Gasket Company?" he asked.

In a moment a very respectful voice replied, "No, sir. No report of anybody."

"I think there may be such a report soon. If so, get in touch with me here."

The Avenger hung up and turned back to the guard.

"Just what did the two men from the truck do when they got inside?"

"The driver," said the guard, "stayed at the loading platform and helped unload the truck. The other man with him, a young fellow with kind of narrow eyes and a mouth a little thinner than most, walked to the employees' entrance. I didn't pay much attention; figured he had a friend working here."

"Then?"

"I turned away. I looked back, and he was out of sight; had stepped inside, I guess. In a minute or two he was at the door again. After that, the truck was ready to go; so he climbed in and went out with it."

"You heard nothing?"

"I heard a kind of muffled thump. That was all. And everything looked all right," said the guard sheepishly, "so I didn't investigate. Which I should have done."

"That must have been when the workman in the employees' entrance was shot," said The Avenger. "Did you examine these men when they drove in?"

"I sure did," said the guard. "Searched 'em from stem to stern."

"How is it you didn't find the young fellow's gun?"

"I don't know," said the man, honestly perplexed. "He didn't have anything on him bigger than a pocketknife. Neither did the other. And there wasn't anything in the truck but just the stuff due here. My pal went over the truck while I went over the two guys."

The phone rang. It was headquarters.

"You must have looked into a crystal ball, Mr. Benson," said a police captain. "We've just had a report of the finding of two men near the Manhattan Gasket Company, in a boarded-up, vacant building. They were slugged, and slugged for keeps. One is dead; the other is unconscious and may never come out of it. No identification."

"I think you will find," said The Avenger, "that they worked for the Atlantic Tool and Die Company. Thank you for calling me."

So that was confirmed. Benson dispatched Mac and Smitty to see if they could find the truck. It had probably been abandoned by now, but there might be vital clues in it. Then he went back to the guard.

"You say there was no one at all in the yard save you and the other guard and the two from that truck?"

The guard started to shake his head, then paused.

"Say! There was one other person. I wonder—" He shrugged. "There was Old Mitch."

"Old Mitch?"

"An old bum who makes his living off the streets and out of junk heaps. Comes around here every so often for what he can salvage. We let him take wood scraps and stuff. Crusty old guy, but he has more spunk than most."

"Was he anywhere near that truck?"

"No," said the guard, thinking back, detail by detail. "Let's see. He was over there by that big crate. The young fella walked from the loading platform past it and—I remember. Old Mitch looked as if he'd like to kill him, and yet as if he was deathly afraid of him, too. Old Mitch hid behind the crate. I don't think the young guy ever saw him."

The Avenger's cold and glacial eyes were unrevealing. He went to his car.

In the plant, he had learned the name of one workman near the time clock who had seen the young fellow from the truck. A man who had been hit particularly hard by the mysterious, slow-motion doom. The Avenger went to the address of that man.

The address was that of a run-down rooming house on West Ninth Street. The man lay in his room, second floor rear, with a doctor in attendance. He gasped for each breath; his color was dreadful. It didn't need Dick Benson's superlative knowledge and skill as a physician to know that death was close.

The doctor in attendance looked up as Dick opened the door, recognized the personage known for treatises and experiments throughout the medical world. They stepped into the hall.

"What do you make of it?" asked Dick Benson, after greetings had been exchanged.

The doctor chewed his lip.

"I don't know, Mr. Benson. I simply don't know. I would swear it was a particularly swift and deadly form of pernicious anaemia. But anaemia does not strike like this, all in a minute. The man is dying, right now!"

"Delirious?" asked The Avenger.

"No. Clear-headed as a well man. But he speaks, and moves, with curious slowness. His motor nerves seem to have been slowed up in their reactions to a fifth of normal."

The Avenger went into the room. The dying man looked up with dumb appeal in his eyes. And Benson's agate, pale eyes contained for an instant their rare look of impersonal but genuine kindliness.

"Can you talk a little?" he asked, quietly, voice like a tonic in its calm strength.

The man gritted his teeth and nodded.

"You saw the man from the truck, near the time clock, I understand," said Benson. "Will you describe him?"

The Avenger got the best description yet.

The man seemed about twenty-five or six, but he may have been older. At least his eyes looked older, dark, narrowed, secretive, with a scar or something in the right eyebrow that parted it in the middle. Thin-lipped, average height and weight, smiling as if he always smiled no matter what the circumstances.

"I'm going to take a blood sample," said Benson to the doctor. "Then I think we'd better take this man to the hospital. We may do something." Though he knew there was nothing really to be done.

The doctor went downstairs to the hall phone and put in a call to the hospital. And the man with the icy, pale eyes proceeded to draw a little blood, pale blood from the dying man's veins, into a small bottle.

He was just securing the stopper when the doctor came back in.

"An ambulance will be here in a few minutes," the doctor said.

The few minutes passed, and far off there was the wail of a siren. The doctor didn't hear. Only Benson, with his miraculous sense of hearing developed in a hundred wilderness and arctic places where he had wrested a large fortune before he entered the crime field, caught the distant, sighing sound.

"The ambulance," he nodded. But then he stopped and listened again.

There had been a faint sound of bells mixed with the siren noise.

At the same moment his nostrils, keen as an animal's, caught the scent of smoke—that deadliest of all smoke—with a smell of wood and varnish and rags mixed in. Then there was a sudden commotion from downstairs, and a frantic pounding of feet as the few in the house began stampeding for the sidewalk.

"For heaven's sake—" gasped the doctor.

And from downstairs drifted the dread cry: "Fire!"

The Avenger was already at the door.

At that moment the stairs were clear enough so that he could have leaped through flame and smoke to safety. But his quick eyes saw at once that another thirty seconds would make the staircase an impossible path. He could get away; but the doctor and the sick man couldn't!

He turned back into the room. And even as the door shut against the searing heat and choking smoke, the stairway became an inferno down which no man could go.

And the stairs were the only descent possible from that floor.

CHAPTER VII

Truckful of Trouble

To find one light truck, among New York's thousands of light trucks, after that truck has left a place nearly an hour ago and mingled with the teeming traffic in heaven knows what direction, would seem an impossibility.

But The Avenger's indomitable little crime-fighting crew was geared in unusual ways to do unusual things. Mac and Smitty had a system. They felt that, though the odds were against them, they had at least a forty-percent chance of locating that vehicle.

At this part of the city there was a newsstand at practically every corner. The two went on foot to the next corner. Since the street in front of the factory was one way, east, that was the way that truck must have gone first, since the driver would scarcely care to make himself conspicuous by breaking laws.

Practically every newsboy in New York knew The Avenger and his aids. This one recognized Smitty by his vast bulk. Often the boys had helped, their sharp eyes and quick wits making them invaluable.

But this time Mac and Smitty drew blank. When Smitty described the truck they were after, the boy confessed that he hadn't noticed it, though it must have passed his stand. There are so many trucks in New York.

So then, Mac went north on the intersecting street, and Smitty went south. Later, one of them would go on east and inquire. But that wasn't necessary.

Smitty called Mac with his little belt radio, which was a tiny transmitting-and-receiving set, so small that it would fit in a curved metal container, worn at the waist.

"Struck oil," said Smitty. "Back to this corner. The truck went south along here."

Corner by corner they followed the truck's progress, at each intersection with Smitty going east or west on the one-way west or east street approached, and with Mac going straight ahead.

There were two things that would have licked them, and which made the odds at least sixty percent against them.

One of these two things was the possibility that eventually the truck would get to one of the warehouse sections that hadn't as many newsstands as in the city proper. The other was that the truck might leave the island by bridge or tube and so lose itself.

The first seemed to be the one that finally happened.

One last newsboy, staring with awe at Smitty's gigantic frame, directed them down Eleventh Avenue. And then there were three long blocks with neither boy nor cop nor peddler's stand that might have witnessed the flight of the brown closed truck.

"Sunk!" said Mac gloomily.

The Scot was the most pessimistic soul alive, usually. The only time he broke his pessimism was in situations so deadly that any other man alive would have despaired. Then in a crazily contradictory way, Mac positively chirped with optimism.

Smitty had come in the huge old coupe he usually drove. He and Mac were in it, now, driving slowly up the last-named street, Eleventh Avenue.

"We'll never find the truck, now," Mac went mournfully on. "But then, we didn't have a chance from the beginnin'—"

He stopped as a hand like a dredge clamped over his left arm.

"Look," said Smitty. "Isn't that the truck?"

Mac stared east, as Smitty indicated.

There, half a block down and parked in front of a huge building that Mac recognized as the side wall of a great wholesale dry-goods firm, was a small truck. The truck was closed, and was brown in color.

"Well, maybe it is," shrugged Mac. "No harm in trrryin', Smitty."

Smitty turned the nose of the heavy coupe, and it rolled toward the truck.

Well over an hour had passed since that truck had left the Manhattan Gasket Company's gate. It must have gotten to this spot forty-five minutes ago.

Neither Mac nor the giant Smitty had the foggiest notion that there might be somebody in or with the truck, after all that time. Why would crooks stay with a stolen car for over three quarters of an hour before abandoning it?

The answer was that ninety-nine times out of a hundred they wouldn't. But the hundredth time they might have foreseen exactly what was scheduled to happen here: a search of the truck for clues so exhaustive that the faintest trace of a fingerprint might be damaging. And that hundredth time they would go over the thing themselves, to eradicate clues, taking as many minutes to the job as their caution thought necessary.

The coupe rolled up toward the rear of the innocent-looking parked truck. Smitty slowed and was ready to stop.

"If we can just find a little sign as to where these skurlies might have gone from here—" Mac began.

59

And then the truck seemed to become one compact engine of death and destruction.

The rear doors swung open, and not one, but two submachine guns blasted at the coupe. Not one, but three grenades were tossed at the coupe.

The windshield was of bulletproof glass; but while it didn't break, it certainly cracked. In five seconds it was covered with white patches and so irradiated with a million little cracks that you could no more see through it than you can see through frosted glass.

Smitty was blind, as far as seeing ahead of the car was concerned.

Then the three grenades went off!

One, landing right beside the car, exploded with a roar that could be heard for blocks. The coupe, weighing nearly three tons, leaped like a feather, sagged to the left and almost tipped on its side, then subsided.

The other two didn't make much noise, but from them came a thick cloud of chlorine gas! And, because the day was windless, the gas just hung there.

The coupe, under its harmless-looking exterior of shabby paint and used respectability, was built like an army tank. That was why Smitty liked to use it.

But even the coupe could not stand this sort of concerted attack. It would be disabled in a few seconds. But Smitty meant to use those seconds well.

There was no time for him to yell a warning to Mac, but the warning wasn't needed. There was rarely need for words between The Avenger and his aids, or one aid and another, in a tight fix. They worked like parts of a harmonious machine.

So Mac instinctively hung onto the edge of the seat with his left hand as the coupe, with Smitty's foot to the floor on the accelerator, roared like a wounded rhinoceros straight ahead!

Smitty couldn't see anything, but he remembered where the rear of that truck was; and that was the target of his mad plunge.

He made a bull's-eye!

The heavy snout of the coupe jammed into the rear of the truck with a roar almost as loud as that of the grenade explosion. And with the moment of impact, Mac had the door on his side open and was rolling out.

His right hand had darted for the door handle, when his left clung to the seat edge in Smitty's dash ahead.

He hit the street a half-second before the giant was out his side, but that was all. Both were on their feet together and leaping ahead so that they would have the blank side walls of the truck between themselves and whoever was inside.

The object of that charge with the coupe had been to knock everybody in the truck off his feet and to cork the rear opening so the men would be penned in there.

It only half succeeded.

The two saw, as they raced past, that the interior of the truck was like an overturned ants' nest, with no telling how many men scrambling over each other to try to get to their feet again.

But the coupe's snout had not plugged the rear of the truck body. The doors were still open, and there was ample room to get out over the coupe's hood.

Which the men proceeded to do!

Smitty saw, cursing their luck, that there were at least a dozen of them, picked up somewhere en route from the gasket factory to this spot.

The men split up, half streaming toward the front of the truck to get at Smitty, the other half taking the other side to get at Mac. And one remarkable thing about them was that they made no sound. There were no excited calls from one to another to do this or that thing; to get those men; to do anything at all.

They acted like deaf-mutes.

The men were firing as they ran. Smitty and Mac both jerked this way and that under the impact of slugs, but neither fell. That was because of their bulletproof undergarments of a substance invented by The Avenger and called celluglass. The stuff was transparent, fine as heavy silk, and with more bullet-stopping power than any steel. Each of Benson's little band wore one, always.

So Mac and Smitty were kicked around considerably— but did not fall, since none of the slugs, fortunately, got them in the throat or head. And the attackers, faces black with rage, stopped shooting and used brute force.

And there they miscalculated.

Twelve men against two, but the two were Fergus MacMurdie and Algernon Heathcote Smith.

Smitty was struck by a human wave an instant before Mac was. He howled with something like berserk delight and grabbed a throat with each hand. His hands twitched, the heads atop the throats suddenly leaned in horrible off-direction, and then the two men were flung bodily at the rest.

On the other side of the closed brown truck, Mac was swinging those bone hammers he called fists. A driving right broke the jaw of the man owning it, and that man subsided into pained quiescence. A left made almost in the same breath draped another man over the doughty Scot's fist like a limp rag over the end of a pole.

From there on, however, it was not so easy.

Mac got in four more hard blows that dazed but did not disable, and then he went down under a human steam roller of sheer numbers. Almost happily, he wrenched at legs, pounded up at faces, and jerked his sandy-thatched head around to try to avoid a rain of blows from fists and clubbed guns.

Opposite him, Smitty was teaching the four men remaining on their feet that odds of four to one didn't necessarily mean a thing.

He smashed a man in the shoulder with a mighty left, and that man crawled off with a broken collar bone. He drove straight through the guard of another man and smashed the head behind the guard. That fellow sagged too.

The other two stopped dancing around. Their actions were those of first-class boxers as well as rough-and-tumble fighters. But what good does it do you to know the science of fighting when you're up against a man-mountain who doesn't bother with boxing at all but just drives steam-hammer blows through any guard you put up?

One of the two had the presence of mind to try to use a gun again. He leaped back four steps and leveled the automatic with which he'd been clubbing around a moment before.

Aimed it, this time, at Smitty's head!

Smitty roared like a bull elephant, picked up the other man and shoved him straight ahead. And it was this man who took the shot.

The man screamed, grasped at his chest and fell. And the one remaining out of six stared, then ran with terrified jerks of his straining mouth.

By now, police sirens were sounding from every direction. At least three squad cars were racing here from different parts of the section.

The men pounding at Mac redoubled their efforts, saw the giant coming apparently unscathed, from the other side of the truck, and they showed their heels right then and there.

So the cops got there and saw something resembling a battlefield in the late evening, with two men responsible for all the carnage. But they arrived too late to do anything but stare, and then to take the human wreckage to headquarters.

They also took the truck for the intense, microscopic examination Mac and Smitty had intended to make but were in no mood to do now. They wanted something besides monotonous routine.

Mac looked at the neighborhood, and then looked at Smitty. They both dismissed from their minds the plate-sized bruises on their torsos where bullets had been stopped from piercing but not from kicking like so many mules.

They were not so very far from the noisome alley on which was the rear-house where Old Mitch dwelt. And Smitty and Mac had been near enough when The Avenger questioned the guard to have heard him mention Old Mitch.

"Let's go," snapped Mac.

So they went to the rear-house.

Just what they expected to learn, neither could have put into definite words. But one of those men back there, one who had gotten away least harmed by the fracas, had been the fellow Old Mitch had sullenly admitted was his no-good son. Both Mac and Smitty were positive of that. There was a chance in a thousand that the son might have gone to the father's hovel to hide, or that the father, angered finally beyond all parental protective instincts, might give some information about him.

But nothing like that happened.

This time Old Mitch was there when they knocked. His feeble voice called: "Come in."

It was the first time the two had been in that room. And their pity for Old Mitch grew.

The outside of the shack was bad enough. The inside was infinitely worse. This room showed cracked plaster and lath, and paper years old was half peeled from the walls. There was a broken chair, a propped-up table, a pallet of rags, and that was all in the way of furnishings. The one bit of working equipment was the rusted, cracked, ancient stove for which the old man gathered the wood scraps.

© Lorillard 1973

Micronite filter.
Mild, smooth taste.
America's quality
cigarette.
Kent.

King Size or Deluxe 100's.

Try the crisp, clean taste of Kent Menthol.

The only Menthol with the famous Micronite filter.

Old Mitch lay on the pallet, now. He blinked up at the giant Smitty and the Scotchman with surly dislike in his rheumy eyes.

"Back again, eh?" he snarled. "I thought I told you I needed no help from anybody."

"I'd say ye were somethin' more than mistaken," Mac retorted, staring at the shivering old body and the green-gray face—where the straggly whiskers showed a face. "Mon, ye're sick again. Verrra sick. Ye should be in a hospital—"

"I'll thank you to keep your nose out of my affairs," barked the old bum. Then his tone softened a shade. "I know these attacks. They go away without doctors. So you can just forget what seems to be my illness. Why did you come here?"

"Because of your no-good son," Smitty said bluntly. "You were in the yard of the Manhattan Gasket Company this afternoon, weren't you?"

"Yes," said the old man sullenly. "I get wood and other scraps there. The guards are kind."

"Well, your son was there, too, as you know very well. And shortly after you left and he left, there was the devil to pay."

He told of the catastrophe at the factory, of the slow deaths sure to result, some indeed having already resulted. And the old man listened with glazed horror mounting in his pain-filled eyes.

"Your son caused all that," said Smitty quietly. "The police and Secret Service, every law officer in the land is now hunting for him. I think what he has done releases you from any parental obligation. If you know where we can find him, I think you had better tell us."

"He wasn't there," panted Old Mitch.

"Look," said Smitty patiently, "half a dozen people saw him. The guard saw you slink away from him as if you were afraid of him. We know he was there."

"He wasn't!" Old Mitch's voice was hoarse, gasping, but determined. Above everything else, his tone and manner said, he was protecting the individual who happened to be his flesh and blood. "I'll swear in court, anywhere, that I didn't see him in or anywhere near that yard."

"Doesn't it mean anything to you that he's the murderer of innocent people?" flamed Smitty.

"You're lying!" panted Old Mitch, with a stubbornness worthy of a better cause. "He wouldn't . . . he couldn't have! He wasn't there!"

The old man wouldn't talk, and neither Smitty nor Mac felt like turning him in for his pathetic loyalties.

So that was that!

CHAPTER VIII

Phony Firemen

The Avenger had returned to the room of the boarding house with no intention whatever of just sacrificing himself with the dying man and the frightened doctor. And he returned, incidentally, just in time to keep the doctor from jumping hysterically from the window and probably killing himself.

"Wait a minute!"

The Avenger's voice was as calm as cold water.

Benson whipped open vest and shirt. Meanwhile, the flames below were crackling more loudly. No natural fire could spread like that. Thermite must have been used.

From his waist, The Avenger took a coil of rope. Rather, the coil looked less like rope than like thick catgut. It was made of the same stuff as the bulletproof garments, celluglass. An eighth-inch strand of the stuff would hold five hundred pounds.

Benson went to the window and looked down. Flame was shooting out the window below. No help that way. He stared upward.

The roof of the next house showed through smoke, a story above this window. There was a parapet, and on the parapet were ornamental knobs at regular intervals.

With flying fingers, he fashioned a noose. The noose rose lightly upward, seeming to have intelligence of its own. It found a knob and clung.

"When I get up there, tie the cord under the sick man's arms," said The Avenger.

The doctor nodded. Benson went up the rope.

Few men could have gone hand-over-hand up so small a cord, even slowly. Such was the steely strength in Dick Benson's average-sized fingers that he went up almost as fast as if it had been a full-inch cable.

"Now!" he cried, over the roar of the fire.

The doctor carried the sick man to the window and put the cord around his body under the arms. Benson hauled him up.

Then the doctor held on himself.

He was hauled up to the adjoining roof as if he weighed no more than a baby. And he found Dick Benson not even breathing hard as he stood with him on the roof.

"Now it's easy," Benson said, calmly.

They went to the edge of this roof, away from the burning building, and the ground showed clear. Men and women in a growing crowd saw them and yelled; but the cries died as they saw Dick lower a limp figure, wrapped in bed-clothes. It was obvious that the situation was well in hand.

The crowd received the sick man, and then the doctor, when he was lowered. And with a final blare the red car of the fire chief arrived from one direction and a small chemical truck from the other.

Men attached the one reel of hose to the nearest hydrant, as The Avenger slid down the rope himself. Then they raced toward Benson as he was twitching to get his cord up and over the parapet knob so that it would fall into his hands.

Benson turned, but not very warily. There didn't seem any reason to be wary.

Even off guard, he almost got sufficient warning. But not quite.

He saw that the suit of the fireman nearest him, who was running with the hose, fitted him so badly that it was almost comical; and in that instant Dick knew that these were no firemen but part of the very gang that had started the fire.

He knew that—and was caught!

With a swiftness and dexterity almost worthy of The Avenger himself, the man twitched a loop of the flattened fire hose around Dick's leaping body.

And down the line, the man at the hydrant turned the water on.

The crushing force of ordinary water! The immense incompressible energy of it! No human being could have torn free from the inescapable grasp of that fire hose, as it filled with a rush from the fire hydrant.

Benson tore at it as one would at a great snake. But even his steely fingers could not loosen it.

He felt his chest contract, his ribs tighten inward. He fought for breath and couldn't get it. He lashed out with his fist at the man holding the end of the hose and could not reach him.

Crowds, roaring blaze, everything faded before his blackening sight. He fell!

The crowds had gaped at the fast attack where no attack would be dreamed. They began to roar as the fire chief's car and the small chemical truck pulled the fantastic trick of suddenly racing away from a fire, with sirens screaming and bells clanging—and with The Avenger on the floor of the red car.

But Benson did not know these things. He didn't know anything for quite a few minutes. Then consciousness returned, though he did not yet open his pale, deadly eyes.

In the first place, he wanted to overhear anything his

captors might say, while they still thought him unconscious. In the second, he wanted to see if any bones were broken or cracked from that terrific embrace, before drawing attention to himself. Attention that was sure to be violent!

The first reason for pretending unconsciousness did not get him anywhere. Once, he did open his eyes enough to flick a gaze around through interlocking lashes. Three men were in the car with him. He saw the backs of two in front, and the feet of a third next to his head. The bells and siren told that he was still in the fire chief's car.

But not with the chief, nor his men. They had undoubtedly been slugged somewhere and their car and equipment and uniforms taken.

However, none of these three said anything that The Avenger could overhear. They said nothing at all, not one word. Now and then, the man in the rear leaned over—Dick could feel the movement—and tapped one of the two in front, probably in some directing gesture. But there wasn't a syllable spoken. The men might have been deaf and dumb.

The Avenger fared better with his second reason for lying low for a time. A cautious flexing of muscles and a slight movement of limbs, as if with the movement of the car, indicated no bones fractured. His chest was sore, but that was merely from bruises.

The red car's siren stopped. Benson felt it wheel over hard as it rounded a sharp turn at high speed, then heard a hollow sound underneath and felt darkness through closed eyelids all around as it jammed into a small garage, a hiding place of some sort.

The Avenger was lifted from the red car and dumped roughly onto cement floor, with grease sliding under his limp hands. Again, he risked a slight look around.

The men, still without saying anything, were rapidly shedding uniforms and putting on street clothes.

Now, with the three busy with clothes and hopping around on one leg and then the other while they put pants on, would have been the best time for Dick to try a get-away. If he didn't try now, the odds were that he'd be unable to later on.

But he waited just the same. It was Nellie Gray's theory that her chief courted death rather than avoided it, and this instance would have confirmed that idea once more.

It seemed like sure death to wait. But The Avenger nevertheless decided to. He might learn something if he allowed himself to be carried farther, or he might locate one of the lairs of this gang.

They piled him into another car in the garage, an ordinary sedan. And then they were on the street again. This time the course was decorously slow, and there were no bells or sirens.

Still, the men said not one word. The Avenger lay in the bottom of the car, slackly, rolling with the sedan's swerves. In a short time it stopped.

The Avenger felt the car sag as the man next to the driver got out. He heard five or six steps on cement sidewalk, then heard a metallic rumble like low thunder.

Dick Benson knew what that was.

It was a garage door of the steel, roll-up type. A garage door to be entered by a ramp across the sidewalk. This, the second stop, was almost certainly the end of the line. And it was almost equally certain that if that door ever rolled down again, with Benson behind it, it would also be the end of the line for him!

The Avenger sat up like a snake uncoiling.

So perfect had been his pretended unconsciousness that the move must have struck the man in the back seat like a movement from one dead. At any rate, his open mouth and astonishment-laden eyes indicated it.

There was a second before he had sense enough to snap the gun he held into line with Dick Benson's head.

That second's lapse was too bad for the man!

With a left hand like a blacksmith's vise, Dick caught the fellow's gun wrist. The gun squirmed inexorably off line, and the shot drew a choked gurgle as evidence that the man had shot his own pal, who had started to turn in alarm from the steering wheel.

Dick's right fist flicked upward with careful precision. It caught the man on the law and knocked him out as surely and deftly as though he had been anaesthetized.

Men were pouring from the opened garage door. The Avenger caught a glimpse of a large, cavernous space with a truck or two in it. He caught that glimpse as he jerked the dead man away from the wheel and leaped over the back of the front seat to take his place.

He gunned the motor and the car started to roll.

Either these men were braver than most thugs, or they had heard of The Avenger's cardinal trait: that he never, under any circumstances, took the life of a human. They jumped in front of the sedan which was roaring ahead like a juggernaut.

Benson jammed the brakes. If he hadn't, bodies would have been tossed like broken wreckage in the car's wake; and, quite possibly, sheer weight of dead human flesh would have stopped him, making violation of his principles fruitless, after all.

Before the car had entirely stopped going forward, there was a clash of gears, and it darted back on its own tracks.

The men who had been inside the building were all out here, now, making the place a good spot for Benson himself to be in.

He roared back over the sidewalk and into the garage, like a crab scuttling backward from attacking enemies. Before the sedan had quite screeched to a stop, Benson was out and hauling down the door.

Even for his lightning swiftness, there was barely time for the maneuver. As it was, the fleetest among the silent men reached the door, and his face grimaced death from a space about three feet wide from sidewalk threshold to the bottom of the steel sheet.

He drew back just in time to keep from having his neck broken. And Benson clicked the lock in place.

Calmly, he went to find a telephone. But before he found one, to dial police, he knew that his risk had been taken in vain.

This was no gang lair to raid. It was a legitimate place of business, "borrowed" by this gang just as they had borrowed the fire chief's car and the chemical truck. Half a dozen bound truck drivers and warehouse men told that story wordlessly even before gags were removed and they sputtered forth the details of being slugged and tied.

Dick was to have been executed in here, at leisure and gang convenience, after which they would leave and never see the place again.

Once more The Avenger had drawn blank. But the glare in the pale, deathly eyes told that this defeat wasn't going to stop him any more than men and machines could stop him.

CHAPTER IX

Creeping Death

The relationship between huge Smitty and petite, delicate-looking Nellie Gray defied analysis. To the eye, it might have looked as though they almost disliked each other. The little blond grenade was always ribbing the big fellow, and he was always snapping back.

But the rest of The Avenger's little band had noticed long since that if little Nellie got into a jam, big Smitty acted like a frantic mother elephant till she had been rescued again. And if Smitty suffered reverses, little Nellie buzzed around like a frenzied, and quite dangerous, hornet till all was normal with the giant.

In fact, it looked as if these two liked each other very much, though steam winches couldn't have drawn that admission from either of them.

Now, Nellie was just about going crazy because Smitty was in very serious trouble indeed.

Smitty was sick.

To say that Smitty was sick was equivalent to saying that the Washington Monument had just fallen over on its side or that the capitol dome had collapsed. Smitty just didn't get sick. He was seemingly made out of scrap steel and old leather and well-seasoned rubber; he might get hurt but he never got sick.

But now he was ill, though still dragging around on his feet; and Nellie was almost going insane with worry.

Smitty's sickness was precisely the same kind as that which had afflicted a lot of workmen in three rubber factories. And as far as was known, that sickness inevitably ended in death!

The affected rubber workmen were still slowly dying, half a dozen or so a day; and the combined medical skill of the country seemed unable to diagnose their malady, let alone cure it.

Sure, slow death. And now Smitty had it!

"Mac, we've got to do something!" cried Nellie.

Mac was as worried as the fragile-looking little blond. But he shook his sandy-thatched head in despair.

"What can we do? If even the chief can't find out what's wrong—"

And that incredible thing had happened. Dick Benson was probably the finest physician and diagnostician alive. And even he had been unable to tell just what was wrong with the giant.

Anaemia of some new, rare sort.

That was a certainty. Dick had been robbed of that bottle of blood which he had taken from the veins of the dying man just before the fire had been started at the rooming house. However, since he had taken the precaution to draw a little blood also into a small rubber bladder, worn next to his armpit for just such emergencies, the loss of the bottle hadn't amounted to much.

He had analyzed that blood sample in every way known to the scientific world at large and also a few known only to himself.

Anaemia. Destruction of the red corpuscles. Very well. But how could anaemia, usually a gradual process, be induced with such lightning speed?

Smitty was not in bed. He was up and around. At the

76

moment he was in the big top-floor room at Bleek Street with the others.

Dick Benson sat at his desk, eyes pale holes in his face as the brain behind them sought to wrest an answer out of this mystery. Smitty walked toward the desk, moving so slowly that Nellie almost cried. His moonface was drawn, and his eyes were dull.

"You ought to be off your feet," said The Avenger. And few had ever heard such gentleness in his voice as there was now.

"No sense in that till it's necessary," said Smitty, words coming slowly and laboriously. "Any ideas, chief?"

"A few," said Benson. His flaming, colorless eyes were fixed on the distance. "You were at the Manhattan Gasket factory. You might have gotten this there. But Mac and I were there, too, exposed in just the same way, and nothing has happened to us. Also, there have been watchmen there since the thing happened, and they have been all right. So I don't think that's the scene of the trouble."

"That rear-house—" said Mac.

Benson's black-cropped head nodded.

"You two called on Old Mitch. He was ill again, as you said he was the first time you saw him, when Josh tried to help him. Quite possibly, the unfortunate old fellow was stricken at that factory with a touch of the trouble. So perhaps you got it from Old Mitch, Smitty. But Mac was there, too, and he's all right."

For just an instant, so fleetingly that not even The Avenger caught it, there was a grim look in Mac's eyes. But he only said:

"I wasn't as near the old man as Smitty."

Benson nodded absently, flaming brain so intent on problems that he was scarcely aware of his immediate surroundings.

"Again and again, threads lead back to that squalid rear-house," he mused. "Twice the old fellow living there

77

has been ill of the same malady as these workmen—"

He paused suddenly, then slowly went on.

"The old man's son seems to be centrally involved in the mystery. And now, in his room, Smitty gets the same ailment."

Josh Newton said quietly: "It looks as if the source of that disease, or whatever it is, is so close to Old Mitch that he has become a victim of it himself."

"In any event," nodded The Avenger, "the place warrants closer investigation." He looked at Smitty. "Go to bed, now. That is an order. And, Rosabel, you be his nurse."

Rosabel Newton, Josh's pretty wife, who was as smart and well-educated as Josh himself, nodded.

"Awww—" said Smitty.

. But the pale eyes did not relent; so he went meekly out, moving like a thing in a slow-motion picture, with Rosabel beside him.

The Avenger turned to Mac.

"Mac, I want you to go to the rear-house and get a picture of one of the occupants. Any one of them will do. Come back as soon as you can with it, and we'll develop and enlarge it at once."

On the near corner of the street intersection down from the alley on which was the rear-house, there was a newsstand."

The boy tending it was one of the few youngsters who did not know about The Avenger. But he was a sharp-eyed lad, and the dour Scot with the bleak but honest eyes won his confidence in a moment.

"Sure," said the lad, "I know that falling-down old packing box where Old Mitch lives. Boy, if a fire ever got going on that crate—"

"Do you know who lives in it?" asked Mac.

"Yeah! I've seen all of 'em coming and going enough to get wise to the layout. There's four rooms, see? Two

78

upstairs and two down. They're all rented. The two upstairs have outside stairways in the back, so each can have a private entrance. One stairway comes down on the left side to a kind of walk to the alley, and one comes down the right side to another walk. And each of the two downstairs rooms has its door."

Mac nodded; he had observed those four entrances for the four rooms.

"Old Mitch lives in the right-hand room downstairs," the boy continued. "Over him lives some woman. Scrubwoman, I guess; she looks like it. Downstairs on the left, there's a guy I've only seen a coupla times. But I know about him. He's a pick-pocket. Johnny the Dip, he's called. Over him is a guy who buys papers from me. He has a twisted leg and works in an office somewhere."

Mac nodded again. It all checked with what he knew, except for this Johnny the Dip. That occupant, he hadn't known of before. But that explained the massive locks on the one door, the portal beside Old Mitch's.

A crook would quite logically have heavy locks to stall any unexpected raid till he could destroy evidence.

Mac thanked the lad, told him to say nothing of the questioning or of his presence around there and went into the alley.

It was nearly dusk, now. And in the alley it was quite dark.

The dour Scot went to a point beyond the rear-house, which was without lights anywhere, and settled down on his haunches behind a barricade formed of two battered refuse cans.

He drew out a small camera that was the finest made and which had several of Benson's ideas incorporated in it. The result was a camera to turn a photographer green with envy.

To the camera, Mac attached a small battery flashbulb. He waited, unseen there; and as he waited, he went over the short list of occupants in his mind. An old tramp, who could hardly be called a tramp as long as he had the determination to house himself with his own efforts, no matter how squalid his shelter was. A woman who looked like a scrubwoman. A bookkeeper a cut above such a neighborhood, but living in it so that his wife could rid herself of lung trouble in Arizona. And a pickpocket.

Quite an assortment.

The old man had inadvertently gotten a touch of the malady from which workmen were dying like flies. At the gasket factory? Possibly. From his ingrate son, who dressed well and drove a new small car but gave his old father blows instead of support? Perhaps, though there had been nothing wrong with the son at that factory. From one of the other three in the rear house? That seemed the most logical of all.

Mac tensed. There had been steps in the alley toward the street. One of the occupants of the rickety house was approaching. He looked over the two refuse cans.

It was dark, but his eyes were accustomed to it. Dimly he saw a dapper figure coming toward him. The figure went to the door beside Old Mitch's, and there was a clink as many keys jangled on a key ring.

Johnny the Dip.

Mac stood up, deliberately making a noise as he did it. The man at the door with the massive locks whirled in alarm.

There was a blinding flash, and Mac had a perfect picture of the fellow, face-on, at close range.

And also, abruptly, Mac had a whole lot of trouble on his hands.

Men suddenly appeared in the alley as if they had sprung from the very cobbles. Johnny the Dip was yelling, but these men made no noise. Like deaf-mutes, they closed in on Mac!

At first, they made no effort to use guns. Quite obviously, noise was the last thing they wanted. They waded in, five to one, with bare fists instead.

It was the kind of fight that would ordinarily have delighted Mac's gloomy soul, for he loved nothing better than to tear and batter with bare hands at the human rats he had dedicated his life to thwarting.

It did not delight him, now. The thing that had tightened his lips and put the grim look in his eyes back at Bleek Street, a thing he had been aware of for several hours, was really hitting him now.

The slow-motion doom!

Mac had picked it up in Old Mitch's hovel, or wherever, along with Smitty. Only it hadn't affected him as swiftly as it had the giant. Mac was a sick man, too, and the sickness showed in this fight.

He got a man in the jaw with a right hook so slow that the fellow saw it coming in time to duck a little and was not knocked out.

He got another in the stomach and doubled him over, but not for keeps. He swung a third time and missed his target completely. And then they had him down.

Only the darkness saved him.

They were trying to kick his head and hammer it with blackjacks. Hands tore at his throat. Other hands ripped at his pockets and his clothing. Nothing bigger than a dime could have escaped the search.

Only the darkness saved him? Well, that was true for the moment. In the end, the real savior was the newsboy at the corner.

The lad heard Johnny the Dip's first yells and ran to the alley mouth. All he could see was a struggling, silent knot, but that was enough. His shrilling whistle was as loud as any cop's, and it brought the Cops in a hurry.

Mac swam back from semi-unconsciousness to consciousness to find a burly cop on each side of him, helping him stand erect.

The Scot's clothes were ripped and ready for the ragbag, because of the violent search the gang had made for the flashlight camera. Everything on him had gone in that search.

But the camera hadn't gone!

"Just a holdup in the darkness of this alley," he mumbled. He was tempted to tell enough to have Johnny the Dip hauled out of the adjacent rear-house and taken to headquarters for a work-out. But he had an idea The Avenger was not ready for a raid on the place, yet. So he did not mention it.

The cops helped him out of the alley and to their squad car. But not before Mac had retrieved the camera which the deaf-mute gang had obviously been willing to commit murder for.

He retrieved it from one of the refuse cans, into which he had tossed it right after snapping the shot. Then he went, walking like a figure in a slow-motion movie, with the helpful police.

CHAPTER X

Blood Killer

Dick Benson conducted one final test on the blood sample taken from the dying workman. It was a test that few of the big commercial laboratories were equipped to make—a test for molecular structure.

In that test, The Avenger had discovered a curious thing, but one which did nothing to clear up the mystery. The molecular structure of the red corpuscles was different from the norm. But what that difference meant, he still didn't know.

"I'm beginning to realize," he said to Nellie Gray, "that we've met the most intelligent of all our adversaries. Somebody is a genius, even if a warped one."

"Still no hint?" asked Nellie. Her soft red upper lip was caught between her white teeth. Smitty was ill, three hundred pounds of rebellious invalid due to die—unless some clue to the nature of this dreadful ailment could be discovered.

"Still no real hint," said Benson. "All I know is what everyone else knows. It is a form of anaemia hitherto unknown. That is proven by the way the red corpuscles have disintegrated."

"Well," said Nellie, "leaving aside for the moment the problem of what this is—how could it be spread through a whole factory in a few seconds and affect every soul there?"

Benson replied: "It did not affect every soul, in every factory."

Nellie's lovely blue eyes asked the question that her lips did not.

"In one factory," said Benson, "just one department was affected. In another, the factory was affected, but not the general office. In the third, office, plant and everything else was affected."

Nellie's eyes kept on asking questions. The Avenger took three diagrams from the top drawer of his desk.

The diagrams showed three factory buildings. One was Wardwear's central plant. Another was Quill's main plant. The third was the Manhattan Gasket Company's plant.

"These lines," said The Avenger quietly, "show the ventilating systems."

So then Nellie got it.

"Blown through the air ducts!"

"Definitely!" said Dick. "Wardwear's plant has four separate circuits, one for each floor. Quill's has one big system, which, however, takes care of only the plant. He never bothered to put ventilating into the general office space. Manhattan Gasket has a system taking care of the entire building."

"It checks perfectly," said Nellie, nodding her blond head.

"Yes. One floor at Wardwear, the crude-rubber department, was affected. The plant but not the office force at Quill's was overcome. At the gasket plant, all were knocked out. In each case, it follows the ventilating circuits. Ventilator fans in rubber factories are very powerful, in order to take care of the rubber dust, so the unseen peril was swiftly scattered in each case."

"What unseen peril?" demanded Nellie.

Benson shook his head.

"And how was it introduced into the ventilating systems? The man in the truck at the Manhattan plant, for instance, was searched before being allowed in, and nothing was found on him."

"It would seem that the search wasn't as thorough as it should have been," retorted The Avenger.

"You were going to inject some of that blood sample into a rabbit," said Nellie. "Did you?"

"Yes," said Benson. "The results were faint, but unmistakable. Slow disintegration of the red corpuscles. And also, a touch of that slow motion that is so peculiar. Definitely, the motor nerve system as well as the blood is affected. And that is all the experiment revealed."

The door opened.

"Mac!" said Nellie. "Were you run through a nutcracker—"

She stopped exclaiming over the state of Mac's features, worked on by the gang in the alley. Something more important than that was wrong with Mac.

He walked toward Dick, moving as slowly as a man in a nightmare with lead tied to his feet. And The Avenger got to his feet in one flowing move, eyes like brilliant agates.

"You, too, Mac?" he said.

" 'Twould seem so, Muster Benson," said Mac. "But I got the picture you wanted. One of the rear-house residents. An eminent citizen by the name of Johnny the Dip."

The Scotchman reeled and almost collapsed.

So then he found himself shortly in a bed near the one in which Smitty mountainously protested. And up in the big top-floor room, The Avenger walked back and forth from front to rear with eyes so terrible that they made even Nellie shiver a little and with that in his tread which suggested a powerful animal, caged for the first time in its existence.

Smitty stricken—and now Mac. Two of his men afflicted with this thing, as terrible as it was bizarre, and for which no cure had been found. Two of his aids doomed slowly to waste away and die, unless this mystery could be solved.

The fact that, at present indications, the whole rubber industry in the United States might be paralyzed was of less importance to Benson personally than the distress of his two comrades.

"Josh! Rosabel!" he called.

Josh and his pretty wife came to the desk. The Avenger's colorless, terrible eyes drilled them.

"Josh, Rosabel, Nellie—please go to the rear-house again. Josh, you will follow the pickpocket, Johnny the Dip, if and when he comes out. Learn all you can about him. Rosabel, do the same with that bookkeeper. Nellie, watch the woman living there. Get every detail possible concerning those three and radio me when each leaves the place—if they do leave it. But don't any of you go inside! It is increasingly certain that Mac and Smitty caught this thing inside. So you three stay clear."

He didn't finish his thought. Which was: "If anybody is to go into what seems more and more to be a house of death, it will be I!"

Full night, now. And that alley was as black as the inside of a bomb. And it gave you the same breathless feeling of impending disaster that being inside of a bomb would give.

Nellie Gray was as indomitable as any man; but no man, knowing what The Avenger and his band now knew, could have lurked in that alley unafraid. She felt a tendency to shiver as she stood behind the outthrust corner of a tumble-down garage, up the alley from the rear-house.

Josh and Rosabel had been with her, a while ago. The three had taken that spot, even though it was some distance from the rear-house. From there you could see, silhouetted against dim light from the street, anyone leaving the shabby shack and heading for the alley entrance.

Three had left, in the hour and three quarters since they arrived.

First, Old Mitch himself had trudged out, carrying his ragged bundle with the sticks and string dripping from one end. Nellie had reported it to The Avenger over the tiny radio at her waist.

Then a dapper figure, twenty or twenty-five minutes later, had slid from the door next tó Old Mitch's. Johnny the Dip. Josh had slipped after him, reporting first to Benson.

Finally, long later, a figure, limping from a twisted leg, had emerged and gone up the dark lane to the street. That exit had been radioed to Bleek Street, and Rosabel had gone silently after it.

Now, there was just Nellie in the blackness. And in the rear-house was just the one occupant, the middle-aged, heavy-set woman. Nellie's quarry.

Time dragged. Nellie looked at the tiny watch on her wrist and saw ten o'clock pass, and then ten thirty. She was about to look at her watch again when, once more, she heard steps from ahead of her. She stared hard, suddenly tense in the darkness.

She heard quite a few steps before she saw anybody, indicating that someone was coming down the flight of stairs in back of the rear-house and was walking down one of the narrow runways between that shabby edifice and one of the apartment buildings next to it.

The indication was right. A figure came into the alley, shown up by the dim street light far ahead. The figure was a heavy-set woman.

The woman Nellie was supposed to track!

From the compact radio at her waist, she drew a microphone no bigger than a quarter and only a little thicker. "Chief!"

"Yes?" came the cold, calm voice from an equally tiny

earphone. It was almost as though the voice sounded inside her own skull.

"This is Nellie. The scrubwoman, or whatever she is, just left the rear-house. I'm going after her. Will report later—"

And off there in Bleek Street, The Avenger turned from the big central radio cabinet which was always kept tuned to the same secret wave length as the small belt radios.

He picked up a small case that resembled an ordinary overnight bag.

Luck, it seemed, was with Benson this night. Four radio reports on all four of the inmates of the rear-house. And then further reports from Josh and Rosabel.

Old Mitch had gone out, and there was no mention of his return by Nellie.

The pickpocket had left and headed for a poolroom where he still was, since Josh had not radioed of any return.

The man with the limp was in a movie. And now the woman was gone. So the place was empty, and that seemed like luck because The Avenger meant to go through that place from one end to the other.

He opened the case that looked like an overnight bag, and instantly the fact that it was not what it seemed to be became apparent.

In that small case was probably the most complete make-up kit in the world.

The lid held a fine, small mirror. The top tray had dozens of pairs of tissue-thin glass eyecups with different tinted pupils, which Benson could slip over his own betrayingly colorless eyeballs. Then there were wigs of every sort; pigments, tints, pads for cheeks and lips.

The Avenger got out the picture which Mac had taken of Johnny the Dip. He clipped it in the rack next to the mirror. Then, with the reflected image of his own face next to the picture of the pickpocket, he went to work.

Dick Benson was a make-up artist without peer and could, in a few minutes, accomplish a character transformation that might take the make-up department of a major movie studio several hours. Now, with the aid of grease paint and putty, complexion tints and pencil, he miraculously adopted the sharp, rattish face of Johnny the Dip. Black brows, a thin, high-bridged nose, the hard jaw and long, thin line of chin.

The eyes of the man were light-colored, either gray or blue. Because of that and because he intended to be in darkness anyhow, Dick did not use any of the eyecups. But as a finishing touch, he stepped to a great wardrobe.

In there were hundreds of suits, old and new, dark and light, shabby and elegant. He put on a dark suit, for the man in the picture was wearing a dark one. He slouched a little, glanced furtively around and seemed actually to be that man.

It was not as good a performance as The Avenger could give in the line of make-up. In the light, it could be seen that he was not Johnny the Dip. But no human eye could tell, in the darkness in which he intended to work, that this was not the pickpocket.

And that, it seemed to The Avenger, was sufficient.

CHAPTER XI

A Ghost Walks

Under the street lamp, after leaving the alley, Nellie could see the woman a little more clearly. And the clearer view made her pretty doubtful about the value of following her.

She had rarely see a more common, average-looking, inoffensive person.

The woman might have been forty-five or she might have been fifty-five. Rather tall, she probably weighed a hundred and forty pounds, and it was a rather shapeless, broad-beamed hundred and forty.

Her clothes were faded and showed a patch here and there. Her shoes were cracked, and there were whitish traces of soap, which confirmed the guess that she was one of the city's myriad scrubwomen. If so, she might be going to work in some big building, now, though it was a little later than such work is usually commenced.

Her face was thinner than her body warranted, and had only one look on it. A look of tiredness. Altogether, certainly no suspect in this gigantic affair of a whole industry on the verge of being disrupted.

The woman took a downtown subway, getting off at Chambers Street. Nellie followed, staying a safe distance behind while they were both in the train.

The woman walked west, toward the river. And Nellie went after her. And then, in a block containing several shabby dwelling places among the dark buildings of daytime business, the woman suddenly disappeared.

Nellie gritted her teeth and decided that she had lost her. But when she hurried in alarm, she caught sight of the woman again, just closing the outer door of a squat, dingy tenement house.

Nellie lurked across the street.

She was there for a long time, so long that she began to get very worried. Was there a rear entrance to this place, and had she lost her quarry through it? She didn't know. But she was worried enough to find out.

She went to the building, through the outer doorway, up rickety stairs. Half a dozen doors confronted her, all dark. There would be as many more up the next flight.

Nellie drew out a tiny thermometer with a copper case —copper disperses heat and cold very swiftly—and with an ingenious little clip on the end.

She went soundlessly from door to door, touching the clip to the doorknobs, watching the thermometer with the aid of a diminutive flashlight.

That thermometer would register the heat of a candle thirty feet away. When it went up a fraction of a degree, she would have the door most recently opened in this place: the lingering warmth of a human hand on the knob would make it a trace warmer than the other knobs.

She found her door in the rear, on the second floor.

To her dismay, no light shone from under this door. And as she listened, there was no sound from behind it.

It looked as though she had been cleverly thrown off pursuit, in which case that pursuit must have been justified. For no innocent person would have been watchful enough to know he was trailed, or would have gone to such elaborate extremes to throw the trailer off scent.

Nellie looked at the lock. It was pretty simple. With a

hairpin, that tool-of-all-work, and with some of the knowledge gained from her work with The Avenger, she managed to slide the bolt back.

Very slowly she opened the door into a pitch-dark room. Very softly she stepped inside—

And then she should have leaped out again at once. For she got that sure instinct of the hunter that the room was not empty, after all. She could see nothing and hear nothing; but she knew that someone was in there!

However, she had no chance to get out. With no warning of any kind, something smashed down on her head.

She fell!

Nellie had been roughly treated before in her pursuit of the type of criminal who had murdered her kindly archaeologist father and set her on the trail of the underworld. But this was about as hard as she had ever been slugged, and a full quarter of an hour went by before she was able to get to her shapely knees and then to small, uncertain feet.

She staggered back to the door, felt around. Her fingers found a wall switch and she snapped it.

Light from an unshaded bulb, hanging from the center of the ceiling, revealed bareness, poverty—and murder!

The room had a bed, a cracked washstand, several old chairs and a table. And a corpse!

The corpse lay in the center of the room. It was that of a woman, middle-aged, heavy-set, with a lined face and with cracked old shoes, whitened in streaks from soapy water.

For one wild instant, Nellie thought it was the woman she had followed. But then she saw it was another. Killed, almost certainly by the harmless-looking person she had trailed to this building.

And then that "harmless-looking" person had lurked next to the door till Nellie came in, slugged her with intent to murder and fled.

"Nice, gentle female," Nellie said grimly.

She began looking swiftly around, ignoring her aching head. And in about four minutes she had the dope.

The tenant in this room was a scrubwoman, all right. There was an empty pay envelope in the table drawer with the name LEGGITT BUILDING on it. And a memo:

On and after the fifteenth of August the cleaning women will please report for duty at midnight instead of eight o'clock due to requests by many of our tenants who are required to work late.

The woman had her coat on, and her hat was on the scarred table. She had been just about to go out when death struck her.

The woman's name, according to the torn pay envelope, was Abigail Ort. Nellie went out, hailed a cab and hurried to the Leggitt Building.

She had lost the person she was assigned to trail, and she burned to make that up. Also, she had found that the woman was in it up to her neck; so if she could locate her and haul her in for murder, many things might be solved.

She thought the locating might be done if she got a list of people connected with Abigail Ort and checked over them; and it was quite possible that her employers, the Leggitt Building, might know of near relatives or friends.

The night man in the brightly lighted lobby of the thirty-story building looked at Nellie with a good deal of approval. She drew that sort of look from any male under eighty. And the night man was only a little over fifty.

"Abigail Ort?" he said, giving Nellie no time to finish the question she had started to ask. "Oh, yes. She works here. She's up on the eighteenth floor now. If you want to see her, I'll run you up."

"She's up there—now?" gasped Nellie.

"Yeah. Came in about ten minutes ago, a little late."

Nellie crammed back more exclamations. It would seem, remembering that corpse in the tenement, that if Abigail Ort were up there, now, it must be the ghost of Abigail Ort walking.

But then the other answer struck her, and her blue eyes went lighter with anticipated action.

She had struck a hotter trail than she'd dreamed of, in coming here. The other woman, apparently, had killed Abigail Ort in order to take her place this night in the Leggitt Building!

Why? Well, that's what she wanted to find out.

"I would like to see her a minute," she said demurely. "If it isn't against the rules."

The night man would have preened his mustache, if he had had a mustache.

"Rules are made to be broken—for certain people," he said roguishly. Then he took her up to the eighteenth floor in the one elevator kept running all night.

The corridor was fairly well lighted, but it was so quiet and deserted that it gave Nellie a sense of being in a tomb.

"She's probably near the back end," said the guard. "She usually starts there and works front."

Nellie nodded and walked toward the rear of the corridor. She walked slowly, wanting the night man to close the elevator door and leave her alone. But he stayed where he was, looking out the open cage after her.

Then she heard the door clang reluctantly shut. Someone had rung for the cage from the lobby or from another floor. She was left by herself in the glistening tunnel of marble slabs.

There was a sound from the end of the hall, and the last door on the right began to open.

Nellie sped forward like a dainty cat, without sound. Light shone out on the bare hall floor from the office.

A woman backed out, taking her time, not acting as though afraid or in a hurry at all. The light clicked off in the office as the woman's hand found the switch, and the office door almost snapped shut.

But then the woman heard Nellie and whirled. And on her face was no longer the weary, vacant look of a person who has worked too hard for too long.

That look had been sponged off and in its place was the snarl of a tiger.

Nellie charged!

The little blond's rush on this woman, who used her muscles for a living and was at least thirty-five pounds heavier than she, was made without a thought of failure. After all, she could handle most large men with her knowledge of wrestling and jujitsu. Certainly no woman could get the better of her!

So she charged the scrubwoman—and she got the surprise of her life.

The woman threw Nellie!

Nellie slid and sprawled half a dozen feet on the slippery marble floor, and then got up with white rage burning in her slim body. This was intolerable! This—

The woman's hand clubbed out at her, clenched, in a terrific blow. That was the opening Nellie wanted.

She caught the wrist behind the clenched hand and half-turned and half-pulled at the same time. This was to have the heavier woman throw herself by her own momentum.

But that didn't happen, either.

The woman wove off-balance, snatched at Nellie's arm, caught it, then steadied herself and closed ferociously with Nellie at the same time.

Nellie concentrated on getting away. She was barely over five feet tall, weighed very little over a hundred pounds. She was not built for give-and-take, close work. And this raging female who grabbed her was built like a barrel, only harder to dent.

The woman's reddened hands got Nellie's throat. Nellie drove her hands up between the woman's wrists, spread them hard and broke the hold.

The woman crashed Nellie over backward, landing on her with a force that made the little blond see stars. And Nellie got her right hand on the back of the woman's neck in the thumb-and-finger nerve press The Avenger had taught her; she squeezed hard.

But even this didn't do the trick. The woman was wary. With the first feel of those strong little fingers, she squirmed hard. The chance of numbing her with the expert pressure went glimmering and, an instant later, so did Nellie's senses.

For once again, the woman slugged her.

A professional-looking sap appeared in her roughened right hand as if by magic. Nellie's head jerked frantically to the left so that the first blow missed. But not the second.

The second got her glancingly on the temple, and a warm black ocean poured over Nellie, with faint sounds piercing it.

Sounds of running steps, and then a change in tempo of the steps as they fled down the stairs. And, finally, a silence more complete, as the black ocean waved back from over her again.

Nellie reeled into the office, clutching her lovely but much-abused head in her two hands. There would be a phone in there. She had to waste precious seconds looking up the official Leggitt Building number, as if it were an address totally outside this place. And then, when she rang the lobby phone, there was no answer. The night man had taken this moment to be somewhere else in the building.

Nellie heard the clang of the elevator door down the corridor outside. She turned to run to the door and halted just a moment.

In this office there were two desks, two chairs, a water cooler and a big filing cabinet. That was all. The tops of the two desks were bare, save for an envelope that lay conspicuously on the one nearest the window.

The envelope was blank, with no writing on it at all, but was carefully sealed and bore something within.

So Nellie took it.

Then she ran to the elevator.

The night man beamed at her in fatherly fashion, but with just a hint of that mustache-preening look and said:

"Did you find her, miss? Did you—"

Then he stopped, because then he saw what had happened to his pretty passenger.

Nellie's pancake hat was over one ear, her hair was disheveled, her clothes were ripped, and her left leg showed a streak of ivory white through a stocking that had an inch-wide run in it.

"Down!" snapped Nellie. "Quick! She took the stairs. She might not have reached the lobby yet. Take me down, quick!"

She started to get into the elevator and found an arm suddenly barring her progress.

"Oh, no!" said the night man, with no fatherly kindness in his voice, now. "No, you don't. I'm not giving you a chance to pull no tricks and get away."

"That scrubwoman," said Nellie urgently. "She isn't Abigail Ort. You didn't look closely enough when she came in. She murdered the real Abigail Ort and almost murdered me. Down to the lobby, I tell you—"

She stopped. The look on his face told her that nothing she could say would move him.

Nellie was in such an urgent hurry that she would not have turned a hair at taking the obstinate man's elevator away from him and going down herself. But she didn't try that, either.

There was suddenly a gun in the night watchman's fist.

"You'll stay right here till I call the cops. No telling how many offices you've busted into and robbed."

"But—"

In the man's not-too-keen wits were stirring accounts of bobbed-hair bandits and beautiful lady murderers and other melodramatic perils.

"You stay till I phone the cops," he repeated. "If you try to get away, I'll plug you, miss. And I ain't kidding!"

He took her, wild but helpless, back to the end office whose door was open, then called headquarters.

CHAPTER XII

The Rear-House

When The Avenger had delegated Nellie and Josh and Rosabel to check on the movements of the occupants of the rear-house, he had ordered strictly that none of them go inside. That was because of the probability that lingering death, in some mysterious form, lurked in the shabby place.

Dick never let his assistants take chances if it could be avoided. He felt solely responsible for them, and fear for their safety was the only fear he knew.

Fear for his own safety, he didn't know at all. In fact, as has been said, he acted as if death would be a thing to welcome rather than avoid.

So none of his aids was to enter that place of slow death. It had to be entered, but the entering was to be done by The Avenger himself.

He went to the place swiftly after Nellie's report that the woman had left. That report had meant that all four occupants were out, and he could have the place to himself.

Like a shadow, or a silent gray fox, Dick got to the alley mouth unobserved by any pedestrian. It was an almost eerie trick of his. He could go down a fairly crowded street in such an unobtrusive manner that no soul could later recall that such a person had passed among them.

And certainly none could recall what doorway or areaway he chose to enter. On this street were only a few people, so the task was even easier.

He went down the dark alley like a wraith, losing himself in darkness so thick that even his colorless eyes, as fine in darkness as a feral animal's, could barely pick the way. And if he had been seen, what of that?

He wasn't The Avenger; he was Johnny the Dip, with a right to be slinking down this alley.

Continuing with that thought, it wouldn't be out of character at all for him, as a reputed pickpocket, to look stealthily around before entering his door, so Dick Benson did that, too.

Catlike, he went past the rear-house, listened, looked into every place in the stubby blind thoroughfare where a person might hide, and satisfied himself that no soul was around to observe him.

Then he went more openly to the rear-house.

The locks on the door of Johnny the Dip were going to take time, so Dick went past them and to Old Mitch's door. The lock there was so easy that he opened it almost as readily as if he had used a key.

He stepped into blackness and shut the door behind him, holding the lapel of his coat over mouth and nostrils as he did so.

His coat lapels, as always, were saturated with an odorless chemical of MacMurdie's devising that absorbed, for a time, the lethal effects of almost every gas known.

Whether the hideous, slow-motion death was in the very air or not, even The Avenger didn't know. But he took no chances. He breathed through the protective lapel.

His flash bit into the darkness of the room.

The first thing Dick looked for was a possible old doorway, boarded over or nailed, perhaps, that might lead into the room next door. In that way, he could avoid time spent on those massive locks of Johnny the Dip.

But there was no such opening; so he went on to the rest of the room and found exactly nothing to rouse any investigator's interest.

There was nothing in the old stove but a few ashes, still warm, where Old Mitch had cooked his dinner with the wood he gleaned from the streets. There was nothing in a cracked and drafty closet but some clothes too near the ragbag properly to be called clothes.

The battered table had a drawer, and in this were some tin knives, forks, spoons and a can opener.

An orange crate, used as a bureau, held a few pitiful personal possessions, probably found in some trash can.

There was nothing in Old Mitch's room to indicate where he might have picked up the slow-motion malady.

Benson went out, around the building, then up the insecure outside stairs to the room above, the one used by the woman who had been trailed by Nellie Gray.

In here, The Avenger moved more cautiously, as there was built up in him a feeling so faint that it had not begun to be apparent till he was just leaving Old Mitch's room. A feeling that was now growing within him by the second.

A feeling of impending doom!

Dick Benson had made his large personal fortune in the wildest parts of the uncivilized world, much of it when he was still in his teens. He had faced death so often, in such varied forms, that he could almost smell it.

And without one tangible reason for feeling that way, he felt death very close to him, now!

It seemed to walk with him in the darkness, step for step. It seemed to gibber behind him and to jog his elbow whenever he stopped. It seemed to claw out for his throat with shadowy but inescapable fingers.

But with pallid, flaring eyes expressionless, he went on with his searching.

He found so little in the scrubwoman's room that the

very scarcity of it was, if the sudden glint in his colorless eyes meant anything, an important clue.

There was one dress, patched and worn, on a hook. There was a hat on the same hook. And that was all.

No dishes, no eating utensils, no little personal things and no linen, save the pair of torn sheets on the sagging cot. There was practically nothing in here to indicate that it was the home of a human being.

Benson went down the stairs, and up the other flight to the room of the bookkeeper with the twisted leg. And his eyes glittered like moonstones in bright moonlight as he found much the same state of affairs here.

Keeping the chemical-saturated coat lapel over his face, he moved soundlessly about.

There wasn't as much stuff in the place as you would usually find discarded, in an empty room, after its tenant had moved out. Bare walls, bare floor, curtainless window.

There was just one room of the four unexplored, now. The room belonging to the character The Avenger was impersonating, Johnny the Dip.

He went to that.

First he moved the door gently, or tried to, because even a hard shove did not suffice to make it quiver in its solid jamb. And that was odd, for the panel looked so old and frail that you'd think a breath would split it.

He turned his attention to the locks.

Dick Benson could pick any lock made, just as he could open any safe made. But some of the latest and best are tricky.

These surprising locks, on a door that looked so frail and was solid beyond imagining, were of that sort. And there were three of them.

Even The Avenger had to take time on those locks, over ten concentrated minutes apiece, to be exact. Half an hour, with the feeling of death mounting yet higher in his breast, and with the more practical anticipation that one of the four living here might return at any moment mounting, too.

But none had come back by the time the third lock opened with a click that could not have been heard by any but The Avenger's sharp ear. He turned the knob and the door, moving so ponderously as to suggest that it might be of wood-sheathed metal instead of plain wood, opened a half inch.

Even the other ground-floor room was not so dark as in here. And even those marvelous pallid eyes, that seemed able to match the sight of an owl in the night, could make out nothing.

As he had done in the other rooms, he stepped inside, shut the door noiselessly behind him and stood a moment with every sense alert, listening.

It was cleverly done.

They must have literally held their breaths when the door started to open, because Dick heard no breathing in that crowded half second of time. They must have had their hands already up, for he heard no sound of clothing rustling.

Not till the upheld arms came down and, with them, a thing like a net that swathed Dick instantly in its paralyzing folds like the tentacles of an octopus!

He heard the preliminary rustling, then, and started to leap ahead.

His whipcord body collided with two other bodies in the blackness, and one of the two went down. But the net went down, too, over Benson more tightly than ever.

He had just one arm free. That was all he had gained by his inhumanly swift leap. But that one arm was worth several ordinary arms.

He made out a dim white blotch which was a face, and his fist laced into it with a force that jolted his arm clear to the shoulder. Another dim blotch showed to the right.

His hand slid around it to the back of a neck, and his fingers pressed the nerves there that induce unconsciousness as easily and smoothly as if an anaesthetic were being administered.

The unseen crew in here were not idle while he was doing this. They were drawing the ends of the net together, precisely as if Benson were some extremely dangerous fish. And through the mesh of the net they were trying to find his head with clubs and blackjacks.

But that one free arm continued to be an amazing menace.

It crashed a blow into another face! It caught the wrist of one of the hands pulling a corner of the net tight, and there was an incoherent, animal-like snarl following the snapping sound of a breaking bone.

Then there was the noise of smashing glass. And right after that, somebody opened the door again. The whole mob, trying to subdue one netted man, squeezed out to the dark alley. The door slammed and the three locks, unhurt by Benson's work, clicked closed.

Something in that room was too fragile and too valuable to risk being smashed in a fight.

They saved more breakage of mysterious glass, if that was the idea. But otherwise they didn't seem to do so well by themselves in the maneuver. In squeezing through the doorway, another end of the net had been wrenched loose by hands that were rather small and white and slim, but seemed made out of tool steel.

At first, in spite of the fact that these men acted without a word to each other, you could fairly feel their almost careless self-confidence. One against eight or ten. The outcome was certain!

Now, still without a sound being uttered by any of them, there was an equally perceptible lessening of that confidence.

In the first place, three men had stayed behind in the

black chamber, reducing the odds materially. In the second, their dangerous and supposedly securely netted fish had now freed his other fin.

In the darkness of the alley, The Avenger suddenly ducked to the cobbles, grasped a pair of ankles and hauled. The owner crashed to the cobbles, too, and was swiftly drawn forward.

How it happened, no one there could have quite told, save The Avenger himself. But eight seconds later, Dick Benson was sliding down the alley like a gray cougar, while behind him a fight raged on that was just as fierce as it had been before.

The murderous crew still had a fish in its net and clubbed on and on at it without having any way to know that the recipient of the blows was one of its own number, dragged under the net after being tripped by the ankles.

As Benson reached the alley mouth, the savage but subdued sounds behind him stopped. The substitution had finally been discovered.

The Avenger dropped efforts to be unseen and unheard. He drew out a regulation police whistle and blasted the night with it.

The driver of the squad car that came racing in answer stared with disbelief when The Avenger introduced himself as the legendary Richard Benson. Dick was still in the image of another man; but a long look into the pale, icy eyes convinced the cop, and he got more excited than he would have in a fight with bandits.

"Round up any men you find in the alley," Dick said quietly. "Then break in the door of the rear-house with the three big locks on it."

"And?" said the cop deferentially.

"There may be men in there, too. Arrest and hold them. Search the place and see if you can find anything at all unusual."

"You are coming with us?"

The Avenger had intended going with them. But not now. For while the squad car was coming, he had received a message from Nellie. A message not of words, but of light taps in code with her fingertip on the tiny transmitter at her waist—a method of sending messages used by any of them when they were not free to talk.

"Held for police eighteenth floor Leggitt Building. Important developments. Can you come?"

CHAPTER XIII

The Gathering Web

Benson went fast to the Leggitt Building, not because Nellie Gray was in any sort of trouble—she wouldn't be where police were concerned—but because he had the idea that Nellie had stumbled onto something too big for her to make decisions about. She wanted him to come before she said anything, even to the police, which might better remain unsaid for a while.

The Avenger's idea that Nellie wasn't held on anything really serious, like murder, was confirmed at the lobby entrance of the Leggitt Building. There was a cop there, but he leaned negligently against the building, looking placid and uninterested.

"Yes, sir," he said to Benson. "Eighteenth floor. That's where she's held. Dunno what she's done. Guess she's a thief or something."

On the eighteenth floor there was even less interest. The night man of the building was arguing with a bored plain-clothes man.

"But what'd she do?" the plain-clothes man was asking impatiently.

"You say she had a row, maybe with this cleaning woman. And the cleaning woman ran away. So what? Do

109

we turn out all of headquarters when a couple of dames have a row?"

"Search her!" bleated the night man. "She must have stolen something."

"That's a job for a police matron, buddy," said the plain-clothes man. "If she did take anything, it can't be very big." His eyes went admiringly over Nellie Gray's lithe form, to which modish clothes clung very snugly. "O.K., we'll take her in if you insist—"

The plain-clothes man saw Dick Benson, then. The Avenger, on the way over, had removed his guise of Johnny the Dip.

"Mr. Benson!" he exclaimed.

"I heard that one of my friends was in a little trouble here," said The Avenger quietly. "Perhaps you will let me vouch for her."

"Say, any friend of yours—" began the detective. Then he literally gaped at Nellie, and afterward at The Avenger.

Dick Benson's aids were only a little less known to the police than The Avenger himself. And they had almost as many official privileges.

"This girl—" said the plain-clothes man. "You—why, say! This must be Nellie Gray!"

He whirled to the night man.

"Why, you dope!" he stormed. "Thief! Steal something! I oughta break—"

The watchman retreated back toward the elevator, with the detective right after him.

"We'll stay up here a moment while Miss Gray catches her breath," said Benson. "I'll ring for the elevator when she is all right."

The cage went down, with an angry detective still berating a subdued watchman. Benson turned to Nellie.

"The woman from the rear-house is in it up to her ears," said Nellie. "On top of that, she is a killer. She murdered the real cleaning woman, supposed to take this floor of the Leggitt Building, about an hour ago."

"You trailed her here?"

"No," said Nellie. "She slugged me at the other woman's place, over west of here. I only came here because I thought I might get information on the dead woman from her employer." Nellie felt tenderly of her head. "And here, big as life, was the woman from the rear-house."

"She killed the real cleaning woman and came here herself?" repeated Benson. "She wanted very badly indeed to get into this building and out again without its ever being known, I should say. I wonder why."

"I think," said Nellie, "she came here to get this."

She drew from her dress the plain envelope she had taken from the desk in the end office.

"Came to get it?" said The Avenger. "She was going into the office, then, when you caught her?" he questioned.

"No, she was coming out."

"Then she must have come to deliver the envelope, not leave it. Though she may have taken something away with her, too."

The Avenger's voice halted. He had been opening the envelope calmly as he talked. Now, he held the contents, a large sheet of paper crowded with figures and symbols.

"What is it?" asked Nellie, knowing it must be something pretty important from the glitter in the diamond-bright eyes.

"As far as a swift glance can tell," said Dick, "this is the missing secret formula for making the tubing gaskets at the Manhattan Gasket plant!"

Nellie stared at him, her own eyes brighter than usual.

"I should say the woman is in the thing!" said The Avenger. "She put this envelope here for the man who rents the office to pick up in the morning.

"And she committed murder so no one could ever trace her visit to the place. Perhaps she merely meant to stun the woman so as to take her place; but, if so, she hit too hard and it's still murder."

"Then whoever is the tenant of this office is in on it, too!" exclaimed Nellie. "I wonder who that is."

"We'll try to find that out first thing in the morning," said Dick. "Meantime, we can look around this office for anything that might tell a story."

Nothing, however, did tell a story.

The office was very much like the rooms The Avenger had looked through at the rear-house, with the exception of Old Mitch's. That was, it had practically nothing in it to indicate that it was used at all.

There was blank paper in the desk drawers, with a bottle of ink and couple of ordinary pencils and pens. There was a half-smoked pack of a common brand of cigarettes in the top drawer of the other desk, the one with the typewriter on it. The cover of the typewriter was so dusty that it seemed not to have been taken off for weeks.

"The office is just a blind," decided Benson. "It was used only rarely for the receiving or sending out of such things as this formula, though the formula must be by far the most valuable thing ever to come in here. Just a blind. But there's still a chance that we can trace the tenant."

At Bleek Street, Benson put the formula in his finest vault, on the first floor of his headquarters building. Then he went on up to the vast top floor with Nellie.

Josh and Rosabel were there, waiting; and the Negro couple had a sheepish look on their faces.

"That shaky little pickpocket lost me," Josh admitted. "I followed him to a poolroom, as I reported. I waited outside for what seemed an hour. Then I got uneasy and went in, and he wasn't there. There was a washroom with a window, and the window was open."

"The bookkeeper lost me, too," confessed Rosabel. "I don't know if it was on purpose or not. He went into this movie, and I couldn't get in after him fast enough to see where he was seated; so I waited outside till the show was over and another half through. Then I went down the areaway beside the theater. One of the ushers was at an emergency exit sneaking a smoke, and he told me a man with a limp had gone out that door a long time ago."

They looked so distressed that Nellie almost laughed. She knew the reason they had been so easily lost, though they were such expert trackers. Neither of them had expected that his quarry would know anything about being trailed, and hence had expected no efforts to lose him.

"Don't worry," she said soothingly. "The pickpocket and the bookkeeper are cleared, I guess. We know the real crooks, now. One is that cleaning woman living above Old Mitch. The other is a man who has rented a certain office in the Leggitt Building. Isn't that right, chief?"

But The Avenger seemed not to have heard. The look in his eyes, making them seem as hard and bright as slits in chrome steel, showed that he was deep in thought.

The thought expressed itself in slow, musing words, in a moment.

"How," he said, "did the men at the rear-house know I wasn't the man I was supposed to be?"

"Huh?" said Nellie.

"I went there as the pickpocket whose picture Mac took in that alley. I didn't make up as completely as might have been done, but in poor light that would never have been noticed. And the light at the rear-house was not only poor, it was nonexistent. It was pitch dark in there. Yet, the moment I opened the door, the men in the pickpocket's room attacked me. They knew, somehow, that I had no business there. Yet, it was utterly impossible for them to see me clearly enough to know that I was not the man who lives there."

"Maybe Johnny the Dip got back before you," said Nellie. "Josh admits he lost him at that poolroom. And if Johnny the Dip was in the room, then anyone else coming in couldn't be Johnny the Dip and would be attacked immediately.

"That's possible," said The Avenger. "But I think I saw all the men when we got out in the alley. Very dimly, yet enough to see that they were all big men. None there was taller than I. And Johnny the Dip, Mac said, was only my size or smaller."

"Maybe they heard you picking the locks and were warned," suggested Josh.

The Avenger shook his black-crested head.

"I worked in such silence that I could scarcely hear the rasp of metal on metal myself. No, that's not the answer. It would seem that it was impossible for the men, in the darkness, to know that I wasn't the rightful tenant of the place. Yet, they did know, the instant I stepped inside."

To Josh and Rosabel and Nellie, it didn't seem to be a very important point, after all. But Benson's eyes indicated that to him it seemed very important indeed.

The phone buzzed softly. There was a battery of telephones on The Avenger's desk bigger than that on the desks of any big businessman. This one was a direct line to police headquarters.

"Mr. Benson?" came the voice of the commissioner.

"Yes."

"A report has just been handed to me regarding a raid at a certain back-lot house, which you requested."

"Good. What did the men find there?"

"Nothing!" said the commissioner.

Benson paused a moment.

"There must have been something in the room," he said. "Signs of occupancy, at least."

114

"Oh, yes, there were the normal things," the commissioner cut in. "But you asked for a report on anything unusual that might be found. There was nothing of that type."

"What were these 'normal' things?" said Benson.

The commissioner apparently had a careful list and a completely detailed report at hand. He read off what had been found in Johnny the Dip's room. Just personal stuff—clothing, electric plate for cooking, utensils, a little furniture, a few food staples in a cupboard.

"And that was all?" persisted The Avenger.

"That was all."

Benson paused again. He had heard something in the room, before being dragged out to the alley, that did not jibe with this innocent report. The smashing of glass. And he had formed the idea, just afterward, that he had been taken out of the place to prevent more breakage of what must have been rare and fragile stuff.

"Was there anything broken in the place?" he asked.

"Why, yes," said the commissioner, sounding a bit surprised that Benson should know. "There was a broken bottle of ketchup on the floor."

The Avenger's pale eyes had that bright-agate look. The thing he had heard break had not been any ketchup bottle.

"The men searched thoroughly?"

"They even sounded the walls and the floor," said the commissioner. "In fact, they went so far as to rip up a floorboard. There was only bare earth underneath; that shack has no basement, you know."

"Did the tenant of the place show up before your men left?"

The commissioner said that he had not.

"What is the police record of this Johnny the Dip?"

"He has no record," was the commissioner's rather surprising reply. "The man is not a criminal as far as the police know."

"In the neighborhood," said The Avenger, "it is whispered around that he's a pickpocket."

"Then the neighbors know more about him than the police department does," retorted the commissioner.

"And nothing was found broken but the ketchup bottle?" said Benson.

"Nothing!" said the commissioner.

The Avenger hung up. Brains here! They'd realized he must have heard, and would remember, the smash of glass; so they had substituted a common glass article to be found in explanation.

But where had they hidden the first fragments? And the other unknown, fragile paraphernalia that he had guessed must be the reason they had not permitted the fight to continue in that room?

The rest looked at him. From the glint in his pale eyes, they judged that he had learned a lot in that talk with the commissioner. But he made no move to impart what he had learned.

"Good heavens!" exclaimed Rosabel.

She was in the corner near the teletype on which constantly was gathered all the news of the world.

They stared at her.

"It's happened again! Another rubber factory in Akron just closed down because half the plant was stricken with that strange illness!"

CHAPTER XIV

A Race with Doom

First thing in the morning, Benson went out and headed toward the financial section of Manhattan. He moved even more swiftly than usual because he considered this case the most vital that had yet come to his attention.

The first reason for this was the dreadful doom released in the factories. The rubber industry was demoralized by those catastrophes, now covering four plants. If any more happened, there would be a complete stoppage. And they would stay stopped, too! No workman was going to enter a rubber plant if he felt that sure, slow death would be his if he did. They would stay stopped till this thing was logically explained and the plotters of the wholesale crime apprehended. There would be no rubber products pouring out; and rubber is a sinew of war and there was plenty of war going on in the world.

The second reason was far more important to Dick Benson, personally.

Mac and Smitty were ill with a malady that thus far was known to have no cure, and to end eventually in sure death. This affair of an entire industry being sinisterly, inexorably sabotaged had to be cleared up, and soon, on the chance that something beneficial to their health might result from the solution.

So Benson moved fast that early morning.

His first stop was at the Leggitt Building. There, the rental manager of the building looked up at the sound of a soft footfall to see a man with coal-black hair, a handsome, though sternly calm, face and frightening colorless eyes regarding him.

"I beg your pardon," he gasped. "You wish to see about renting an office?"

"No," said Benson quietly, but with the authority in his voice impressing this man as it did all men, "I am of the police." Which was true enough. "I would like to ask a few questions."

"Yes, sir," said the man.

"Office 1819," said Benson, giving the number of the end office in which the secret formula had been left. "I would like to know whatever you can tell about the tenant."

Whatever the manager could tell was certainly not much. He didn't know the man's business.

"He said he was an importer when he came to rent an office, but he didn't say just what he imported; and it is our policy not to question tenants as long as they are quiet and law-abiding."

His name was Anton Grish. He had rented the place five weeks before and had paid three months' rent in advance. He had not been in the rental office again since that time. There were no complaints of any sort against him.

"That's all you can tell me?" said The Avenger, pale eyes making it practically impossible for the man to lie.

"That's all," said the manager.

So The Avenger went to that fount of building information, the elevator starter.

The starter knew Grish by sight. He was young, had a mouth a lot thinner than most and kept his eyes half closed in a narrowed and secretive way. He dressed pretty well and was excessively quiet, not even responding to any

118

of the elevator boys' greetings, so the starter had never heard his voice.

"Did he come in regularly, every day?" asked Benson.

"Oh, no! I don't think he was in more than once a week. I guess he traveled a lot."

"Quite possibly," murmured The Avenger. He was thinking of Akron, Ohio. "Can you describe him any more closely? Was there anything unusual about him?"

The starter thought a moment.

"There was one thing. A kind of scar, or something, in the middle of his right eyebrow made it look as if it had been parted there by a little comb."

The Avenger thanked him and went on.

So the man who had rented Office 1819 under the name of Anton Grish was the man who had killed two men at the Manhattan Gasket Company and walked out with the secret formula. Then, it appeared, he had quickly gotten rid of the formula till he was sure he wouldn't be picked up and have the thing found on him. Finally, it had been taken back to his office again, for him to dispose of as he saw fit.

The man at the Manhattan plant and old Mitch's black-sheep son!

But now it seemed that he was something more than just a vicious, ungrateful offspring. He was a major criminal, high in the circles responsible for this grim sabotage.

Now, the problem was to lay hands on him.

Up on the eighteenth floor a detective was posted to nail the man if he came to his office. But Benson was pretty sure this wouldn't happen; pretty sure the woman who left the envelope would have contacted him and warned him by now.

As for that woman, she hadn't gone back to the rear-house again. Probably never would go back now. So The Avenger would have to find both of them, with little to work on, in the city's absorbing millions.

It seemed like an impossible job; but this man with the glacier-ice eyes had often done impossible things. All the police in the country had been hunting for Old Mitch's scape-grace son and couldn't find him. It was up to Benson to do it single-handed.

He phoned the Newark airfield. The executive in charge there was quite surprised when Dick arranged to charter a fast small plane. He was surprised because he happened to know that The Avenger had a whole fleet of planes and that most of them were better than anything Newark could offer for hire.

Then Benson phoned the city's most famous columnist, and that person was more than surprised. He almost dropped. As a rule, The Avenger made it so uncomfortable for anyone who insisted on giving him publicity that the unfortunate offender never had the nerve to try it again.

And now, by all that was miraculous, Benson wanted publicity! And on a matter which would have been an exciting scoop even without the addition of Richard Benson's highly newsworthy name.

So the famous column of this famous columnist was hastily changed in the composing room between the early afternoon edition and the late edition. And at the head of it appeared:

What young man with the frostiest eyes imaginable has time and again solved crime riddles beyond the capacities of even the Federal investigators? We give you three guesses but know you'll only need one. And now he has done it again. It was not generally known before, but recently a highly important secret formula for the processing of rubber was stolen. This formula has just been recovered by the man in question, who has chartered a plane to fly down to Washington and to the war department with it tonight. But don't tell

120

him we told you so, because none of this is supposed to come out in the open!

It was about eight o'clock that The Avenger climbed into the small cabin plane they were holding for him at Newark.

The man with the crooked eyebrow had been informed that the formula would be en route to Washington in the hands of his deadliest enemy. And the chartering of a public plane would make it very easy for the man to find out just when, and in what ship, he was leaving. So all was well.

All, that is, from the standpoint of The Avenger.

Any other man would have felt that all was far from well! Because once more in his perilous career, Dick Benson was offering himself as live bait to a ring of killers. If you can't go to the crook, make the crook come to you. It was an effective maxim—but not one conducive to a peaceful old age.

It was a little more than an hour and a half till sunset when Dick took off. If his trip was uninterrupted—that is, if death refused the practically engraved invitation Benson had offered it—he would land in Washington at late dusk.

But he hadn't gone far before he saw that this trip was never going to be completed!

It was a beautiful evening, calm, and the light up there was amber and clear. His plane was winging along the shore line with Atlantic City almost in sight.

And then a soft hum sounded from a tiny earphone held by a headpiece to his left ear.

He had slipped that apparatus on immediately after leaving Newark. It was a little like the earphone worn by a deaf person.

The thin wire trailing from it went to one of Dick's own inventions. It was a sound detector in a case easily fitted into a coat pocket. The detector was so contrived as to be variable in reception. That is, with the turn of a knob, it would become insensitive to any given noise, pick up any other outside noises up to a great distance, amplify them and bring them to that little earphone.

Thus The Avenger had turned the knob till the noise of his own plane motor was tuned out almost to nothing, except, of course, for the direct noise which washed into the cabin from the whirling cylinders. He plastered the earphone tight to his ear and awaited developments.

And here was the sound of another plane motor.

He looked out the side windows and could see nothing. And he was flying fairly low, so it was improbable that the other plane was beneath him.

He rolled a little, and then located the plane, about four thousand feet higher.

Only four thousand feet from him, and his sensitive detector barely caught its two-motored hum. It must be beautifully muffled. And it was gray black so that save in direct daylight it would be very inconspicuous in the heavens.

The Avenger's eyes were as cold as bits of moonlight as he thought that over. He could picture that sinister ship lurking in this country where it had no business to be, slipping silently and camouflaged through the sky, bearing its agents of destruction.

Bearing them notably from New York to Akron, Ohio, and back, in the recent past!

The hum sounded louder in the tiny earphone. And with it came a shriek that meant only one thing: the plane was diving!

With that sound came the first tracer bullets, ripping into the cabin of Benson's ship. Two instrument faces on the dash seemed to explode of themselves, showering bits of glass.

Then The Avenger was darting down toward the sea-shore beneath him, rolling and twisting, performing all the feats known to an expert air fighter.

At this point in the coast, there are long stretches of salt marsh on which there are no buildings, nothing but desolation. One of these bare stretches rushed up to meet Dick, with its long, wiry grass wavering in a slight evening breeze.

There was a faint chatter audible over the road of his motor, and suddenly a ragged pattern of bullet holes wrote itself in the right wing.

The Avenger pulled the nose of his plane straight up. Up he went, in a long loop, and then down at all the diving speed the plane could take, nose to the marsh! The per-forated wing quivered in protest like a shivering animal. And then, just as it seemed he must crash, he hauled back on the controls.

The plane's nose missed the ground by inches, searing the tips of the marsh grass. The plane's tail did not!

Mud and salt water splashed like a geyser as the tail dragged, with Benson fighting the controls with every atom of power in his incredible body, but with his eyes as cool and calculating as though he were safe in an armchair somewhere.

When it could no longer be prevented, the nose slammed down, too, with another geyser following it. The nose and prop caught, the plane angled up and up, then fell over on its back.

There was a darting tongue of fire that instantly became a flaming red curtain. And away from this deadly fire, gliding low through the marsh grass so that it scarcely rippled above him to mark his progress, went The Avenger.

It had been the most skillfully faked accident imag-inable. And swiftly it fulfilled its purpose.

The fast plane came down like a fly for a piece of sugar. Its pilot set her down within a hundred yards of the burning ship as lightly as a falling leaf.

Set her down, but would never be able to take her up again, for this marshy surface was too soft for wheels but not liquid enough for pontoons. Dick wondered about that for a moment. Then he saw four men scramble out of the cabin; and an instant later saw red flame begin to envelope that plane, too.

The plane had served its purpose. Trapped by the marsh, it was deliberately being destroyed so that its identity and secret could never be discovered. It was a commentary on the size of the stakes in this game that a plane, worth many thousands of dollars, would be destroyed with no more thought than the lighting of a match when its function was ended.

The four men from the plane were slogging through the marsh, up to their knees at times, occasionally sinking up to their waists. They made heavy weather of it, but they moved as fast as they could.

And when they reached Benson's plane, though the gas tanks were due to explode at any second, they wrenched open the bent doors and stared in. Then their faces expressed a frenzy of rage and disappointment as they saw inside neither the pilot of the plane nor the secret formula.

Their faces expressed rage, but none of them expressed anything at all audibly. It was as if they were deaf-mutes.

The Avenger, twenty yards away, probably felt as much disappointment as they, though his impassive face displayed nothing at all. For the man he was after, the man with the crooked eyebrow, was not among those four!

All this preparation and maneuvering, and the quarry had been too clever, or too timorous, to fall for it. He had sent underlings after Benson and the formula. So now it was time to deal with those underlings.

The Avenger carried two of the world's strangest weapons, holstered at the calf of each leg.

One was a slim, streamlined .22 revolver, equipped with a silencer of his own devising and far superior to the regulation silencers. This small weapon he called, with grim affection, Mike.

The other was a throwing knife with a hollow tube for a handle which made it blade-heavy, and which was as sharp as a razor and keen-pointed as a needle. This was Ike.

Benson drew both weapons, now. They looked absurdly small and mild compared to the service automatics the four by the burning plane had in their hands.

He aimed swiftly with Mike. A bullet whispered from its silenced little muzzle, and a man went down.

The man was not dead. Benson never took life. He was creased; that is, the bullet had been made, with eighth-inch accuracy, to glance from the top of his skull, stunning him, instead of drilling his brain.

The three men left stared at their suddenly felled comrade with gaping mouths. No one around to club him down, no sound of a gun, just this swift and silent fate.

Another fell, as Mike whispered forth another little slug. And then one of the remaining two caught the other's arm and pointed. He had seen the wave of marsh grass against the wind where The Avenger lay.

The two plowed toward him. It was a reckless act, but there was the crazy light of fanatics in their eyes. As they came, they shot again and again for the spot where the grass had waved!

The Avenger was no longer in that spot. He was two yards to the left. A third time Mike whispered! One of the two went down. Three gone, leaving one.

There was one more bullet in Mike; the streamlined cylinder held four slugs. But Benson did not use it. He wanted this man conscious.

The remaining man suddenly lost his fanatic bravery. He turned and started to run.

Run, however, was not the word to use in that clogging marshland. He floundered more slowly than an average walk. And after him, like a tiger slipping lightly over a surface that mires an elephant, came The Avenger.

But he did not try to catch the man. Not yet.

The shore road lay a mile across the marsh in the direction the man had chosen. Why carry a heavy body when it can get to a destination under its own power?

The man ran, blindly, senselessly, till the road was almost reached. Then Ike, the keen throwing knife, flashed from Benson's hand in a lazy arc. It did not hit the man, it went over his head and came point down in the marsh ahead of him, like a shot across a steamer's bow.

The man stopped, panting, exhausted. Dick got to him and laid a hand on his arm, with the thumb seeking a nerve center near the armpit. The man was trembling with promise of unendurable pain if he disobeyed orders.

He went to the road with The Avenger, under the urging of that grip. Benson flagged a car, taking his prisoner with him.

One prisoner, the sole result of that perilous and beautifully faked plane crash!

CHAPTER XV

Sick Hunter

Smitty felt like the girl at the dance who has gone in the expectation of being the belle of the ball and winds up as the night's wallflower.

Instead of being in the thick of this still-unexplainable mess, he was lying around in bed like a frail baby with the colic.

Smitty had never been sick before, and he was a bit ashamed of it, now. Also he was damned tired of being in bed, even if he did feel like falling over on his face when he tried to stand up.

At the moment he was in the second-floor room with Mac, who lay weakly in another bed across from him, rubbing in the giant's frailties.

Rosabel was not with them. Their pale-eyed chief had just come in with a prisoner, one of the gang they were fighting; and she had gone up to the top-floor headquarters room, filled with natural curiosity, to see if anything was going to be pried out of the man.

So Smitty judged it was a good time for an invalid's rebellion.

He sat up in bed, feeling his head go round and realizing that he was moving with that weird slowness. He swung his columnar legs over the side of the bed.

"Whoosh, mon!" said Mac, words slow and labored. "What d'ye think ye're doin'?"

"I'm getting up," said Smitty painfully. "If anyone around here thinks I'm going to spend the rest of my life in this bed, he's crazy."

"What are ye gettin' up for?"

Smitty was getting his clothes, with slow movements, and putting them on. Putting them on with difficulty. He admitted to himself, as he staggered around like a sick elephant, that he was pretty ill at that. But never would he have admitted it to anyone else.

"I'm going to have another talk with that bum, Old Mitch," he said. "He has to be made to realize what harm he's doing in shielding that good-for-nothing son of his from the police. I'll bet the old guy knows right where to lay hands on him."

"Ye can't have a talk with anybody," protested Mac. "Mon, ye don't realize how sick—"

"I'm not sick at all," lied Smitty. "I feel swell."

"Awww, now Smitty—"

"Are you going to keep your mouth shut?" demanded the reeling giant.

"I'll catch hell when the chief comes down and sees ye gone—and me not raisin' an outcry to stop ye."

"You could have been asleep when I went out, couldn't you?" said Smitty. "Matter of fact, you ought to be asleep right now. You are, aren't you? You don't know a thing I'm doing, do you?"

Mac sighed. "I guess not," he muttered. "But—"

"Sweet dreams," said Smitty, going slowly to the door. It was hard to drag one leg after the other and make them support him.

He shut the door on Mac and went down the stairs.

He didn't take a car, because he knew his reactions were much too slow for driving. He would have hit everything in sight, long before his slow foot could have moved sluggishly to the brake pedal.

He took a cab, with the driver staring curiously at this huge fellow who moved so ponderously and spoke so slowly that there was a two-second pause between each word.

The cab driver stared again when the big fellow told him to stop, and they got laboriously out of the car a block from the alley.

Smitty had felt very smart and rebellious in refusing to give in to his physical weakness when there was work to be done. He had tasted in advance the satisfaction of perhaps locating Old Mitch's son—a thing so urgently necessary—all by himself while The Avenger was busy on another angle.

Now, he felt nothing but doubts as to his physical ability to accomplish any kind of job at all.

But he went on. He was hanged if he'd just go back, having come almost to his destination.

He went on toward the entrance to the dark, squalid alley wherein lay the rear-house, and Old Mitch. But it seemed that the old tramp was not in the rear-house.

As Smitty neared the alley, a shambling, stooped figure also came toward it from the other direction. The figure carried a tattered bundle under an arm. Old Mitch had been out somewhere and was coming in at just about the time Smitty had chosen for an interview.

Smitty lurched slowly toward him. Old Mitch was going to get down the alley before he could reach him. He saw that. But he went on, and he must have looked like a very drunken man, so besotted that he didn't know what he was doing or where he was going.

Suddenly, another figure appeared, a casual pedestrian going the same way as Old Mitch and rapidly overhauling him because Old Mitch wasn't much for lightning movements, either.

The man started to pass Old Mitch, paused, and his hand went to his pocket. He gave the old fellow a coin— Smitty saw the glint of it—and went on his way. He looked curiously at the staggering giant; and Smitty looked down at him and saw just an average-looking guy who was considerate enough to give a pauper a coin.

Smitty got to old Mitch just at the alley mouth, because of the delay. And the old man glared up at him with all his usual surliness.

"You again! Didn't I say I didn't need any of your help?" he snarled.

"Me again," said Smitty, words ludicrously slow. "You take help from people sometimes, though, don't you? That guy back there gave you money."

Old Mitch shrugged.

"From strangers I'll never see again, I sometimes take help, if they offer it voluntarily. Not from busybodies like you." He stared curiously at the big man, and his voice had a different note. "What's the matter with you, son? Had too much to drink?"

"No," said Smitty. "I . . . I'm a little under the weather. That's all. But I want to talk to you."

"What about?" demanded the old man, voice snarling again.

"About that no-good son of yours," began the big fellow.

At once the old man's lips closed tight.

"What about him?"

"I want to know where he is," said Smitty. "We've got to find him and question him."

"What for? He hasn't done anything wrong. I'm sure of that. He doesn't treat me quite as I'd like to be treated, but he's all right at heart. He'd never do anything serious."

"You've heard what he has done and can judge for yourself if it's serious," said Smitty. "You'd better forget your scruples as a parent and remember only the duty you owe all mankind."

Smitty was moving down the alley toward the rear-house, as he spoke; and Old Mitch, hesitating at first, started moving with him.

"I owe mankind a duty!" he snapped bitterly. "Look at me. Look at the way mankind lets me live. To hell with mankind! You don't really think my boy had anything to do with that factory trouble?"

Smitty told him just how thoroughly he thought so, and by that time they were at Old Mitch's door and he was fumbling for his key.

"You're crazy," he snarled unhappily. "My son would never mix up in anything like that. What do you think is behind it? Some foreign power that maybe wants to keep tires and things from being made for the enemy?"

"Something like that," said Smitty, as Old Mitch at last fished a key out and shifted his tattered bundle from under his right to under his left arm.

He stared at Smitty with eyes keener than usual.

"Say! You got something like that factory trouble, ain't you? The same kind of sickness. Where'd you get it?"

Smitty's lips thinned.

"Right here!" he said. "See what all that means? Whatever causes that sickness is in the air here, too. I got it here, I'm sure. A friend of mine, the Scotchman, got it here. And you yourself got it awhile ago! How? It must have been from your own son, proving that he had been here several times, with the police of America all after him."

The old man's hand trembled as he inserted the key in the lock and opened the door. He stepped in, and Smitty followed.

"My boy would never risk exposing me, his own father, to such a thing," he said tremulously.

"He'd risk you with more than that," said Smitty grimly. "He—"

131

The light went on, then, as the old man's finger found the switch. And Smitty didn't say any more.

He didn't say any more because the light revealed that they had company. Half a dozen men were standing in the room; they had been waiting in the dark!

Smitty heard Old Mitch cry out hoarsely and saw him reach for the broken chair to try to use it as a weapon. Then four of the men were on the giant.

It was like a fight between a crippled tank and a squad armed with mobile antitank guns and grenades. The tank still had slow power, but the battle was hopeless from the start.

Smitty swung with what he thought was crushing force and swiftness. And before his slow-moving right arm had leveled out, with its fist supposed to crack a man's jaw, that man had grinningly ducked, lunged and had come up clear behind the big fellow. He got in a full swing with a sap.

It would have downed even a well man; but even ill, the giant was more than a match for an average person. He sagged a little, saw the room go around, but was not knocked out. His hands found the man's leg and he squeezed slowly.

The fellow moaned and beat his hands against the vast paws, out of his mind with pain. And the other three started clubbing.

Smitty's senses relaxed. He felt his hands open and saw the floor coming sluggishly up to meet him.

The last thing he heard was the bleating of Old Mitch in the grip of one of the men. The last thing he saw was a gun barrel coming down on Old Mitch's head, too.

Then he was out of this world and in another where blackness reigned and there was no seeing or hearing anything at all.

CHAPTER XVI

Giant in a Trap

The Avenger's pale eyes had hypnotic powers seldom granted a human. He didn't say anything to his captive, up in the big top-floor room. He just stared deep into the man's mud-brown eyes till he saw them go dull and blank.

Then he commanded the man to open his mouth. The man seemed not to have heard, only looked perplexedly at him; so Dick pried open his jaws himself.

The fellow had a tongue, even if he seemed unable to use it.

The Avenger knew more languages and obscure dialects than perhaps any other linguist alive. He started with the commoner European languages, reaching through them till he hit on Hungarian. The fellow's eyes stirred a little.

Benson began asking the question: "Do you understand me, now?" in such freakish and outlandish variations and dialects of the Hungarian language that Josh and Rosabel stared at him, wondering if he was speaking any coherent tongue at all. And, finally, he got an answer.

"Hungarian," Dick said, "but speaking only an obscure dialect of Transylvania and knowing no other tongue."

So Benson went on in that dialect and answers came with dull obedience from his hypnotized captive. Not very revealing answers, they concerned the man's companions rather than the leader Dick was after.

Many men worked for this leader, a man with a crooked eyebrow. Each man was from a back-country section of a different Central European nation. Each spoke a different language and only that language. Thus, these hirelings could speak to no one, not even to each other, and perhaps spill secrets.

They had come in under quota and reported to this man. But they did no laboring work. They did what this man commanded, which several times had been murder.

The Avenger's pale eyes reflected an icy glint of disappointment. He had cleared up the seeming muteness of the gang: none knew English or the other's tongue, and so could communicate only with each other by sign language. He had established the fact pretty definitely that the sabotage of the United States' rubber industry was the act of a foreign nation at war.

But that was all.

This man knew nothing of the means of sabotage. He knew nothing of the leader, the fellow with the crooked eyebrow, Old Mitch's renegade son. He knew nothing of real value.

There was a buzz at the door and Josh stared at the tiny television set that showed whoever was in the vestibule. It showed a messenger in uniform.

Benson admitted him at once, and took from him a small package carefully done up in oiled silk.

"A new angle on the factory disease," Dick said. "I analyzed the blood of one of the workmen and got nowhere. It occurred to me to analyze scrapings from the lungs, also, since this thing seems to be spread by means of ventilating systems. This is a sample from a workman who recently died. I'll be in the laboratory, Josh, if I'm needed."

Josh nodded. He and Rosabel were the only ones with

The Avenger in the big top-floor room. Mac was downstairs in bed, sick. Smitty was supposed to be in the same place.

Nellie Gray was still out on the trail of that scrubwoman. The woman had simply disappeared off the face of the earth. It was pretty certain she had not left Manhattan. That island, reached only by tunnels and bridges, can be closed promptly and thoroughly by the police. They had so closed it at Richard Benson's orders and were ready to stake their reputations on the statement that no such woman had tried to get away.

But if she was still in Manhattan, where on the island was she?

Nellie had followed every angle and got nowhere. Now, she was on about the last one she could think of. She was trying to trace the store where the woman might have bought the envelope in which that secret formula had been found.

It was practically an endless job; but Nellie was not scheduled to follow the racing very far. It was just after dark, when she turned out of her eighteenth notions-and-stationery store in the neighborhood of the rear-house, that her little belt radio vibrated almost soundlessly as a sign that she was being paged by one of the crew.

She put the tiny phone to her ear.

"Smitty talking. Anybody catching this please answer. Smitty talking!"

"Smitty!" Nellie was furious. "Are you at Bleek Street in bed? And if you're not, why aren't you?"

"I'm not at Bleek Street," came the giant's far voice. "I thought I could do some good by talking to Old Mitch again, and now both of us are in trouble."

"You big—" Her voice broke. "You were in no condition to get out of bed. Oh, if I ever get my hands on you— Where are you? And what's wrong?"

"I don't know where I am," confessed Smitty, voice slow and laborious with the alarming malady. "But there's plenty wrong. Old Mitch and I were slugged by his son's gang, I guess. It looks as if his son is going to commit patricide. We're in a basement. I think at the rear-house."

"There isn't any basement under the rear-house," Nellie snapped. "The police reported that. They tore up some floor boards to make sure."

"Then I don't know where I am. But Old Mitch and I were taken in his ground-floor room at the rear-house. Get the chief. Maybe he can tell, from a look around, where we were taken."

His voice died, and Nellie started explosively for Old Mitch's alley, which was only about six blocks away.

En route, she tried to get in touch with The Avenger. But at that moment Benson was in his laboratory, with his small radio left outside because of certain magnetic experiments he was trying. And both Josh and Rosabel were downstairs exclaiming over the fact that Smitty had gotten up and gone out.

Nellie arrived at the rear-house without having been able to contact any of the others. So she stopped trying and crept soundlessly to Old Mitch's door to get to Smitty on her own hook.

The big dope, getting up out of a sickbed and going to fight a gang of killers when he had about as much strength as a sick calf! She could have killed him. At the same time, without a second thought about it, she was quite prepared to face death to get to his side.

At Old Mitch's door, she stood a long time, in the darkness of the miserable alley. She was listening. Apparently, Old Mitch and Smitty had been ambushed in the room into which she was preparing to go.

She didn't want to be ambushed, too. That wouldn't help the big fellow any.

The little belt radio could be used as a sort of stethoscope, with a hundred times that instrument's amplification, by turning it off wave length, putting one earphone against a wall or door and plugging in a second earphone. You could hear a person breathe through six inches of brick wall with that.

Nellie had this to the door and was listening—and hearing nothing. She was sure there was no one in there. So she picked the lock of the door and swung it open.

She leaped inside and to the right, just to make sure she didn't walk too easily into waiting arms. But still there was no sound so, feeling foolish, she snapped on her flashlight and turned its beam around the empty room.

This was the first time she had been in the place, and its bare squalor shocked her. How could anyone live in a room with dirty, cracked walls and ceiling dripping moisture; with only rags to sleep on, a broken chair to sit on, and a stove made out of an old oil tin in which to burn bits of refuse found in the streets?

But Old Mitch's financial status was not the thing she had come here to explore. She wanted a key to Smitty's whereabouts. She began to look around.

Something glittered on the floor. She picked it up. It was a coin. The coin had been given Old Mitch by the casual stranger on the street just before Smitty had approached the old man; and when Old Mitch fell in here, it had slipped out of a hole in his ragged pocket.

Nellie had no way of knowing all that. But she did know that a man of Old Mitch's extreme poverty would not willingly go off and leave a coin lying in plain sight on his floor! It corroborated Smitty's statement of violence.

She put the coin in her purse and looked around some more. And suddenly she felt hostile eyes on her!

She whirled to the door. It was still closed. She examined each of the four walls. They were cracked all over the place, but no crack seemed to go through and allow anyone to see in. She stared up at the ceiling.

From the center of the ceiling hung the one light bulb which was Old Mitch's entire system of illumination. There was a rusted tin knob on the ceiling from which the wire dangled. And at the edge of the metal wire guard there was a small hole.

With her flash aimed at that hole, Nellie was suddenly sure she had seen an eye, just before that eye had been whisked away. She started to go a little closer to the center of the room, where she would be right under the light cord.

Somebody hit her from the rear! She was crashed to the floor like a football runner with four unblocked tacklers hitting her at once.

She got a whirling glimpse of an open door where there had been a closed door a moment ago. She saw two more men rushing toward her from the alley. Then one of them stepped on her flashlight; there was a grinding noise of glass and the white beam went out.

In blackness, she fought a number of arms that were trying to strangle her and at the same time club her into unconsciousness.

She got one, and her slim white fingers, that looked so rosily frail but were so deft and strong, found a nerve center. The arm wobbled and jumped convulsively in its effort to be drawn away.

She gave another arm a deft twist and heard an incoherent yelp. A hand was over her mouth, roughly keeping back any screams for help she might have had in mind. She used her small white teeth to excellent advantage, cried out once, then was clapped to silence again.

The men holding her must have been the most surprised crew in existence at the amount of force necessary to subdue one small girl. But they had the force, and to spare, with such odds.

One of the swung gun butts, or whatever weapon was

138

being used, clipped her over the ear. And that ended that!

Something rubbing away at her wrists finally penetrated her blackened senses.

It was annoying. It hurt. No doubt the rubber thought he was being gentle and helpful, but it felt like an application of sandpaper, with her skin due to come off at any moment.

"Hey!" she thought she yelled.

Actually, it was hardly more than a sigh, accompanied by an opening of her eyelids.

Smitty was staring down at her, looking worried to the point of lunacy. He kept on chafing her wrists, till Nellie said:

"Stop it! Do you want to saw my hands off? There's certainly one thing you'll never use to win hearts—that's the softness and delicacy of your hide. It's like a washboard!"

Smitty didn't care what she said as long as she said something.

"I thought you were dead," he said.

"Not yet," snapped Nellie. She struggled to a sitting position and looked around.

A windowless cement wall surrounded them. The room it made was very large. The ceiling seemed to be of concrete too, with a square trapdoor or something in the center. A fine line around a large oval on the end wall showed that the door was a massive slab of cement.

Smitty still hovered beside Nellie. At her other side, more gruff now than snarling and surly, was Old Mitch. His rheumy eyes showed more concern than you'd have thought the old tramp had in him to feel for anyone.

Nellie felt exasperated.

"This is a basement. But there isn't any basement under the rear-house. Where are we?"

CHAPTER XVII

Test-Tube Story

In the laboratory, Benson had raced through a series of chemical experiments on the scrapings from the dead workman's lungs so delicate and precise that they'd have made any world-famous chemist exclaim with admiration.

And from the test tubes had emerged a bizarre story.

Also, other bits of the puzzle of the slow-motion scourge had clicked into place in The Avenger's coldly flaming brain. A pattern had almost completely emerged. A pattern so obvious that The Avenger felt icy rage at not having seen it from the beginning, yet knew that he had been thrown off by its very obviousness.

When Dick emerged from the laboratory, Josh knew from the glitter in the pale, dreadful eyes, that the chief had discovered a great deal. And at the question in his face, The Avenger nodded.

"The lung scrapings give the answer," he said. "It explains the impossibly swift, deadly anaemia that seems to attack the workmen and the odd slow-motion symptom that goes with it. It explains everything."

In his vibrant voice was glacial fury, and his colorless eyes were dreadful.

"In the scrapings," he said, "were traces of powdered

benj, rubber dust, emery dust, and an oxide with a single atom of oxygen instead of a complete molecule."

Josh was a highly educated man, but aside from mention of emery and rubber dust, none of this meant a thing to him.

"Benj?" he said.

"A drug made from powdered, baked hemp," explained The Avenger. "It's as old as the *Arabian Nights,* and as evil as Satan himself. The chemical is what caused the slow motion. That stuff acts on the motor nerves, slows them way down, though the person affected doesn't realize that at first. So workmen would suddenly begin feeding machines at only one fifth of normal speed, without knowing it, and the machines would jam or race emptily."

"An oxide with an atom instead of a molecule of oxygen?" blinked Josh.

The Avenger enlightened him a little on that, too.

"An oxide is a combination of oxygen with a metal or metalloid, as a rule. In this case, the combination seems to have been completed with the rubber dust instead of a metalloid. That served two purposes: it gave the oxide the necessary complement and made detection almost impossible because rubber dust is expected to be floating around in a rubber shop. The oxide, as I said, was formed of incompleted molecules. Those incompleted molecules, introduced into the blood stream, instantly sought to combine with more oxygen to become the compound ordained by nature. Just as nature struggles constantly to fill a vacuum, so she always struggles to round out an unnatural or incompleted molecule. In this case, the struggle swiftly robbed the red blood corpuscles of their normal oxygen, producing an instantaneous, synthetic anaemia." *

Josh blinked some more.

---

* The final nature of the oxide was later analyzed in full by Dick Benson, but was never published for fear it might be used again by criminals.

142

"The combination is subtle indeed," said The Avenger. "The powdered emery abraids the lungs. The fine dust of the oxide and the benj is allowed to enter the blood from the lung surfaces. It keeps on seeping in for days, producing the slow motion and the eventual death which we have observed."

"To be effective in an entire large factory," said Josh, "a good deal of the stuff would have to be dumped into a ventilator system. And after the first catastrophe, the plants were well guarded. How could anybody carry a bundle that large and not be noticed?"

The Avenger's colorless eyes were deadly agates.

"A very simple process was evolved for the transportation. A lot of hemp would have to be brought in to whatever laboratory was being used to produce this witch's concoction. The transportation of that was easily solved, too."

"I don't see—"

"Can you remember," said Dick slowly, "seeing a certain person always with a bundle in his arms?"

"A ragged bundle, with bits of string and ends of broken wood trailing from it?" said Benson.

"Why—" gulped Josh. "Why— Say! Yes! Old Mitch!"

"Right! Old Mitch seems always to have a bundle of pitiful odds and ends under his arm. Wood for his old stove, principally. He must have carried in a great deal of fuel in the short time since he first came to our attention. Which is rather odd, since the weather is warm. Surely he doesn't use all that wood for cooking?"

Josh was dancing around as if he had grabbed hold of a shock machine.

"His supplies! Sure! He brought them in in that old bundle—"

"And took them out again in the same bundle," said The Avenger. "Yet it occurred to none of us to wonder why he should be taking bundles out of his place as well as into them. An old tramp, with his toes sticking out of his shoes. Who would suspect anything wrong of such a character? Who would have anything but sympathy for his plight? And under the noses of everyone, he brought in his supplies and took out his finished product for others to distribute."

"The rest in the rear-house," yelped Josh. "They must all be just underlings, with Old Mitch as the boss."

The Avenger's black-thatched head was shaking.

"So many subtleties that it would hardly occur to anyone to delve into them," he said. "Till just a few minutes ago, when I got the answer, there has been one question that has puzzled me more than almost any other. I went to the rear-house disguised as one of the tenants, Johnny the Dip. It was far too dark for even the most miraculous of eyes to have penetrated the disguise. Yet, the moment I entered the pickpocket's room I was attacked by men who knew, instantly and surely, that I was not Johnny the Dip."

Josh stared askance at the pallid, deathly eyes, feeling a tendency to shiver himself, in spite of his long association with their owner.

"Never has anyone seen any two occupants of the rear-house at the same time," Dick said. "We have seen the bookkeeper alone, the pickpocket alone, the woman alone. But never any two together. And now the woman has disappeared as if the earth had swallowed her up."

Josh almost got it but refused to believe it. His face said so.

"In other words," said The Avenger quietly, "there is no woman, no pickpocket—who puzzled the police because they had no record of him—and no bookkeeper with a twisted leg. There is only Old Mitch. They are all Old Mitch, who, I'll wager, is not as old as he seems."

"B-but—" stammered Josh.

"Old Mitch would not want to go in and out of his

144

place too often," mused Benson. "But four people, a house filled with mythical tenants, could go in and out as often as desired with no one paying any attention. Also, any one character could utterly disappear at a moment's notice if something slipped up, including the central one of Old Mitch himself. It must be that. It answers everything, including the question of the attack on me when I went there as Johnny the Dip. The attackers knew I wasn't the pickpocket because there isn't any such person!"

It was then that Josh felt the warning vibration of his belt radio. The Avenger didn't have his on, so he didn't get it. Josh went to the big radio in the top-floor room. A girl's voice was whispering, urgently, warily.

"Josh, Nellie. Go ahead."

"Josh, they've got us in a basement somewhere near the rear-house. Smitty and I, and Old Mitch—"

"Old Mitch!" said Josh. "You mean—prisoner?"

"Yes. A minute ago the gang came in and tied us up. I managed to get to Smitty's radio, and I'm using it now. More men coming. I have to stop talking. But if the chief can locate this place, I think he can catch the whole gang and wipe up the entire affair—"

Her whisper stopped. The radio was dead.

"Come on!" said Benson.

"Old Mitch a prisoner!" exclaimed Josh, as he hurried after the gray fox of a man who could move so swiftly without seeming to exert any effort to do so. "Doesn't that upset everything you—"

There wasn't time to complete the question. Josh ran to keep up. The two shot to the basement in the elevator, and twenty seconds later The Avenger's fastest car roared up the ramp, over the sidewalk and down Bleek Street.

It stopped, in record time, two blocks from the rear-house. The Avenger led the way, with Josh running to

145

keep up, not to the alley, but to the street just south of the alley on which fronted the bigger, better structure behind which the rear-house squatted.

Bigger and better, but only by comparison.

The building taking up the front end of the lot was a boardinghouse type of building with dirt-littered steps on which sat a man in shirt sleeves, smoking a pipe.

The one man was the only sign of life in the place, and he didn't stay there long. As Josh and Dick passed under the nearest street light, he saw them, got up swiftly and started inside.

A lookout posted there!

Josh, like a black snake, darted up the stairs and after him. He caught the man in a dingy hall and swung. He swung hard. There was a sound of bone on bone and the man fell without sound, knocked cold.

"All right now," said Josh in a low tone.

He did not see a face at a door at the far end of the dim first-floor corridor. A face that disappeared instantly when the man fell from the knockout blow.

The Avenger joined Josh and led the way to the rear.

"Basement?" whispered Josh.

"Yes," said The Avenger. "There will be a tunnel."

Josh nodded. It was all clear to him, too, now.

The perfect set-up! In this supposed boardinghouse, any number of the foreign-born men, who acted like deaf-mutes, could stay without rousing neighborhood comment. In the rear, a shack occupied by four people even more poverty-stricken than those in the boardinghouse. And one man, pitied as an old bum who was too independent to ask for help, owning the works.

But Josh was still worrying over the reported fact that Old Mitch, too, was held prisoner.

As for Benson's comment, there would certainly be an unseen method of getting from front to back. A tunnel.

146

Josh's own humiliating experience of losing a man he was trailing proved that.

He had trailed Johnny the Dip to the poolroom, and lost him. Johnny the Dip had come back, had gone in the front building, then through a tunnel to the rear-house. There he had shed the make-up and gone out the rear-house again, disguised as the scrubwoman.

It had been known that the rear-house was watched when Josh and Rosabel and Nellie lurked in the alley. This method had been used to draw the watchers off one by one.

"Here we are," Dick whispered.

An opened door showed stairs leading down. They descended. The basement seemed to be just what the basement of such a building should be—filthy, littered with refuse, with a rusted furnace in the center and stacks of baled newspaper piled perilously near. No one would have looked at that cellar and divined the secrets it held.

The Avenger halted under one of the two lights that hung at each end of the basement. Josh saw then that, dirty as the floor looked, there was actually no dust on it. Refuse, yes; but no dust. That was because dust might show tracks, and tracks might lead to a spot which it was desirable not to reveal.

Nevertheless, Dick bent closer to the floor, and those pale, infallible eyes of his searched slowly over it.

They found a faint line where dust from outside had been deposited by many shoes on the otherwise dustless cement. He followed the line to the rear wall.

"Here we are," he said.

There was a ragged crack that seemed just accidental in the end wall. But if you followed it, you saw that it made a complete, if very rough, oval.

Benson looked carefully along the wall, with his head within an inch of it. At that angle, his almost microscopic

147

eyes saw a faint smudged area around a slight roughness in the cement.

He pressed in the center of the area.

The rough oval swung out. It revealed a dimly lit tunnel in the rock and earth of the back lot.

And it revealed what seemed to be a solid wall of gun muzzles!

Six or seven men were framed in that oval, low, high and higher so that each could get a clear space for a sub-machine gun. They had been silently stolidly waiting. Now, if either Josh or The Avenger moved a muscle, they could be blasted to bits. Even the celluglass garments could not stop machine-gun bullets at this close range, and, besides, some of the slugs would be sure to hit their heads.

The men came slowly out. They circled around the two; then one man jerked his head in a wordless command for Josh and Benson to precede them down the tunnel. They did so. Another solid, concealed door opened. They were thrust into a large basement room with their captors following and shutting the door after the lot of them. And the shutting of the ponderous door was accompanied by a solid thud like the knell of doom.

CHAPTER XVIII

Retribution

"Chief!" wailed Nellie, lying bound on the floor and staring up at Dick and Josh, whom she had drawn into a trap.

Benson said nothing. His eyes expressed nothing. His awesome, paralyzed face was like glacier ice as he let himself be prodded to where Smitty and Nellie and Old Mitch lay.

There had been about a dozen of the silent gang in the room before Dick and Josh were pushed in. They were at one end, by themselves, with guns in their hands but not bothering to level them. The captors of Benson and Josh walked over and joined them, leaving the prisoners by themselves. There was an air of hopeless waiting.

"Tough luck, chief," said Smitty.

The giant's thought was plain in his face. Every one of the little crime-fighting crew carried always the realization that by the very law of averages he would some day get into a jam from which there was no getting out again.

This looked like it!

Since the men in the room seemed to care little what the prisoners did, Dick experimented. He stooped and began to untie Nellie.

149

The men stared but made no move to stop him; so he went on from there. He loosed the bonds of the giant, Smitty. Then, with his slim, steely hands going deftly over the rag-clad body, he untied Old Mitch, too.

Josh was flabbergasted. After all The Avenger had said about the old bum, now he was untying him! And saying no word of warning to Nellie and Smitty!

But Josh didn't utter any words of surprise. He knew Dick always had a reason for anything he did. He must have one here, even if it wasn't at all apparent to the bewildered Josh.

"Thanks," said Old Mitch in surly tones. He sat up, with an effort, and rubbed his ankles and wrists. With no consideration for Nellie, he proceeded to curse the men at the far end of the basement room. They only stared stolidly.

There was still that air of waiting for something.

Suddenly, there was a sound above them. They all looked up.

A hole was appearing in the ceiling. It was a very large hole. The trapdoor that had covered it took up nearly half the floor of the room above. They could see solid bars, that still remained over the hole when the trapdoor was swung wide. And beyond, they caught glimpses of glass laboratory apparatus.

"The room of Johnny the Dip," said Benson calmly.

Nellie stared. "Then we are under the rear-house! But the police ripped up floor boards and found only bare earth—"

Benson pointed. Nellie saw that the trapdoor, now held straight up on edge, was about a foot thick and that it had packed earth between the top layer, which was the rickety floor of the rear-house, and the bottom layer, which was of cement. The cops had taken up a floor board, had seen that bare earth and assumed it went right on down, solidly.

The little band saw somebody up there looking down between the bars over the hole, but they couldn't see who it was. And then the thing that had been awaited happened.

There was a creak, and the door in the end wall, the one through which Josh and Benson had just been thrust, opened again. Now, two more were pushed in. And Smitty groaned when he saw them.

Mac and Rosabel. This gang had broken into Bleek Street and rounded them up.

The Avenger and all his crew were in here, now.

Mac came toward them, moving slowly, dazed and ill. Rosabel helped him. She was disheveled, testifying to the fight she must have put up before being caught.

"Mac," said Smitty, "didn't you have sense enough to—"

"I had sense enough to wait till I was taken," snapped Mac bleakly. "I didn't just come here under my own power, anyhow. I wasn't as obligin' as ye were."

While the door was open, the gang in there handled their guns less indolently. All of them covered their prisoners, so there could be no dash for the door.

At the same time, two of them warily approached the group.

They got Old Mitch, one on each arm, and started toward the door with him.

The Avenger's whipcord body quivered with the urge to prevent that move. But if he had twitched a muscle in rebellion, a dozen guns would have gone off at point-blank range.

"There goes our hostage," said Josh, watching Old Mitch go through the door and understanding the situation at once. "As long as we had Old Mitch with us, we might have been safe. Now—"

"Now it will come any minute," said Dick quietly.

"Old Mitch? Hostage?" mumbled Mac. "What do ye mean?"

So they told Mac and Nellie and Smitty what they meant, and their savage amazement was almost funny.

"Old Mitch himself!" rumbled Smitty. "Right under our noses from the start!"

Nellie exclaimed, and snatched from her purse the coin she had found in Old Mitch's room. On it was scratched, in tiny letters:

August 2nd, Wardwear Plant 3.

"We were certainly slow," said Nellie. "Here is a slow-motion disease, supposedly incurable; yet Old Mitch caught it twice 'by accident' and recovered. He got it from his own poison brew and knew enough to cure it. Yet, we didn't catch on! At least I didn't."

The gang in the basement room, still covering The Avenger and his crew, began backing toward the door in the wall.

"They're clearing the room for action against us," said Smitty. "This is it, all right!"

"Yes," said Benson, voice as calm as his unalterable face. He took a bottle from his pocket. "Each of you take a swallow of this. We'll divide it as well as we can measure it by eye and each take a sixth."

But now something was happening to the gang of killers that drew their eyes. They saw the one nearest the door press the spot that should have opened the solid portal, and they saw that it did not open. The men looked stupidly bewildered, then vaguely afraid.

The man in the lead jammed his thumb on that spot again, and still the thing didn't open. A Babel of outlandish exclamations sounded out, in obscure languages no one of which was intelligible to any but the speaker.

"For Heaven's sake!" faltered Nellie.

"It looks," said The Avenger calmly, "as if the leaders in this affair have decided this is a good chance to get rid of any of their own men who might know too much. Start on the bottle, Nellie. You first."

Nellie shrank back from the bottle with dismay in her lovely blue eyes. The contents of the bottle did not look appetizing. It was the most poisonous-looking stuff she had ever seen, purplish green, looking a little like cylinder oil.

Then, gagging over it, she got down about a sixth of the little bottle's contents. Mac and Smitty, Josh and Rosabel, and finally The Avenger swallowed their portions.

None of them, save Dick, knew why.

The strange Babel of all these killers from the central countries of Europe sounded louder. The men had forgotten all about holding their prisoners at gun point, now. They were all glaring up at the grating in the ceiling.

So The Avenger and the others looked, too.

Old Mitch was up there. And the man with the crooked eyebrow, his black-sheep son.

But Old Mitch had shed the straggly whiskers, and he looked many years younger. The man with the crooked eyebrow wasn't lifting a hand against him now. They were all arms-around-the-neck, the best of pals. And both were grinning as if at the joke of the century, though there was nothing reassuring in those grins.

There was death in them!

"Benson," called the man who had been Old Mitch, "you are supposed to be very clever. Can you guess what is to happen to you, now?"

Never had the face of The Avenger been more expressionless. Never had his voice been more calm than now.

"Of course," he said to the two murderously grinning faces seen through the heavy grating. "You have a favo-

153

rite method of wholesale murder. You will use it, now, on us, as you have already used it on hundreds of innocent rubber workers."

"That's right," said the rejuvenated Old Mitch. "The slow-motion death. I've got enough in my hand to kill a hundred men. More even than the amount I gave my first lieutenant, in the yard of the Manhattan Gasket Company, after the stupid guards at the gate had searched him and passed him. In this small, closed space, no ventilating system is necessary. When this little paper sack breaks on the floor below, the almost impalpable powder it contains will fill the air of the room in less than a minute."

The Babel of the gang, doomed to die as well as the prisoners, became a wild chorus as the men from Central Europe saw the little sack and realized what it meant.

"Cattle!" said the man who had posed as Old Mitch's son. "Time to clean them all out and get new and ignorant ones."

"This sabotage is going on, then?" said The Avenger.

His voice was so calm that the two up there almost lost their grins for a moment. Then the grins came back.

"It will continue," snapped the man who had acted the part of ungrateful son, "till your entire rubber industry is demoralized. It will be applied to other industries, making goods for our enemies in Europe. When it is finished, your country will be paralyzed. But so will our enemies. We shall win, and then quite possibly come over here to pick up the pieces before you can recover."

"That's what you think!" began Smitty hotly.

They saw then why the two had talked. It was to get them off guard so that none would be quick enough to dart forward and catch the little sack so that it should not hit the floor, when dropped, and break.

And, now, drop it did!

It struck the cement with a soft, harmless-sounding

154

little squoosh, and split wide open. From it came a whitish cloud! Dust, powder, so fine that when it began to disperse it became practically invisible.

But each man there knew that it was entering his lungs with every breath—and that it spelled death!

There was bedlam from the doomed gang, paying the inevitable penalty of working for men who killed with no more compunction than murder machines. But there was no sound from The Avenger's little band, though their faces were pale and their eyes wide. They did not want to die. But in the face of death, they were entirely composed.

The two up above were grinning. Their faces started to withdraw from the open grating.

"You!" called Benson. "Old Mitch!"

"Count Franz Bord, to you," jeered the younger man. Their faces were pressed to the open grating again. "The best chemist in Europe. Educated in this country, as I was. Holding citizenship papers, as I do, but with a few affiliations still left in our homeland. What is it that we can do for you, Mr. Richard Benson?"

"You might make your wills," said Dick, almost mildly. "And if you have any last requests to be mailed to your home country, you might leave them with us."

"Bah!" snarled the count who had lived as a tramp. "You talk big. Didn't I tell you there was death for a hundred men in that room? You breathe death every time your lungs work."

"So do you," said Benson, more mildly still. "The dust of death is rising up through that open grating so that you are breathing it as we are. Just to be sure you get your full share, I called to you so that you'd put your heads down to the grating again—into that powdered murder of yours."

A look of supreme contempt came into the man's face.

And a wider grin than ever into the face of the younger man.

"You are naïve, my friend," said the count. "Do you think I could work with the powder without an antidote? Carefully as it is handled, it must infect the handler. So before I used it at all, I worked out the antidote. I shall take it from my pocket in a moment, and we two shall be safe—-"

"Will you?" said The Avenger, with pale death in his eyes.

There was a silence, the silence about a charge of explosive just before it goes off.

Then the older man swore hoarsely in an alien tongue and grabbed for his side pocket. In mounting frenzy, his hands went through the rest of his tattered pockets. And they came out empty.

"You . . . you swine!" he panted. "You knew I was the leader instead of a victim! You took that bottle from my pocket when you untied me down there!"

Benson said nothing. His eyes seemed to reach physically up and pierce the two stricken faces.

"Give me that! Throw it up here or we'll blast you all to—"

"There is nothing to throw, I'm afraid," came Dick's calm voice. At the same time he waved backward with his hand; and his crew obediently moved to a far wall out of vision of the grilled hole in the ceiling. "My friends and I shared the bottle a few minutes ago. All of it!"

The younger man screamed. It was like the shriek of a woman drowning in a boiling sea.

"Franz!" he yelled. "The antidote. He . . . he— Can you get more?"

"No!" The other man's voice was so tremulous that the words could hardly be made out. "There is no more. Only

156

that, which should have been enough. It would take weeks, months, to—kill them! All of them!"

The two began shooting, wildly, insanely. But The Avenger had leaped back to where the rest stood, like a pale-gray cougar. And at that point, the men above could not see. They emptied their guns, reaching down through the grating and firing blindly all around! Several of their doomed gang screamed and fell. But The Avenger and his band were not hit.

Then there were two more shots. Just two, in the room above. They were different in pitch, and they were a little muffled.

The aids of The Avenger looked at each other.

"They preferred a quick death to a lingering one," said Mac, in a low, hushed tone. Through the grating sagged a limp arm. The hand held a smoking gun. The fingers uncurled slowly as they watched, and the gun dropped to the floor beneath.

Nellie sighed.

"They signed their own death warrants. As killers who fight against you always do." She stared at Benson. For the first time since she had known him she saw on his face tiny pin points of moisture. And she knew then what the rest still hadn't guessed.

Not till a moment ago had Dick been sure that was the antidote, which he had taken from Old Mitch's pocket. He had deduced that there must be an antidote, because the man had twice been ill and twice recovered. But he had not been sure, till the two went crazy with fear, that the vile purplish stuff was it—and not some unknown poison.

"The job is done," said Nellie, in a tired, flat tone, weak with nerve strain. "We can break out of here at our leisure. Mac and Smitty will get well. But the others, the factory people—"

"There will be enough droplets left in the bottom of the bottle," said The Avenger, eyes never colder, "for me to analyze the antidote and quickly reproduce it. We can save most of the victims, if not all."

He turned to the horror-crazed outlanders and spoke to each in his own dialect. He commanded them to build a living pyramid, so Smitty could drag himself to the bars in the ceiling, which his ponderous strength could bend aside.